Time Travelers

Another Les Didlin misadventure

By. Will Sanders

Published by Rabid Dog Enterprises

Table of contents:

THIS BOOK IS DEDICATED TO all DUMB ASSES

~~***TIME TRAVELERS***~~

Another Les Didlin Adventure novel

FIVE DAYS IN JUNE, 1876

Early Summer 1876

The Northern Plains Indians faced a predicament. They were all supposed to be on reservations. They weren't happy with that situation. They were being forced off their traditional hunting grounds and were expected to live on rations supplied by the government. Some that had previously resisted were shipped to Oklahoma or Florida. A few more fortunate tribes had been assigned to better locations within or close to their traditional hunting grounds. But as soon a white men discovered they liked these reservation lands they moved in. Then the Indians were moved out to less desirable lands or were forced to cede large portions of land to the whites. Case in point— the Black Hills. This was supposed to be Lakota Sioux and Northern Cheyenne Reservation. Then gold was discovered and the whites moved in. The tribes were being forced to cede the best land to the whites.

It wasn't just the Black Hills. White settlers were gobbling up land all over the Great Plains. Indian tribes were squeezed into smaller and smaller hunting grounds. Those hunting grounds were being depleted of buffalo by hunters, often for just the hides, leaving the meat to rot. Some renegade whites were hunting down and scalping innocent Indians for no reason other than they could. Some renegade Indians were attacking white settlers and stealing horses in response. President Grant had a big problem.

1876 rolled up and the northern plains tribes gathered for a big powwow to discuss the Black Hills problem. Meanwhile the U.S. government decided to get tough and force all the tribes back to the reservations or be shot. Early summer found a very large Indian camp in the Little Big Horn Valley of Montana. They were mostly Lakota Sioux, Northern Cheyenne, and Arapho with some from a few other tribes.

While the tribes gathered the army had plans of their own. Three columns of cavalry and infantry would converge around the traditional summer hunting grounds in the Yellowstone Bighorn area. One commanded by Colonel Gibbon would come from Fort Ellis located near three forks, the beginning of the Missouri River in Montana territory. Another column commanded by General Terry set out from Fort Abraham Lincoln located on the Missouri River in Dakota Territory. The third column commanded by General Crook started from Fort Fetterman down south on the Powder River in Wyoming Territory.

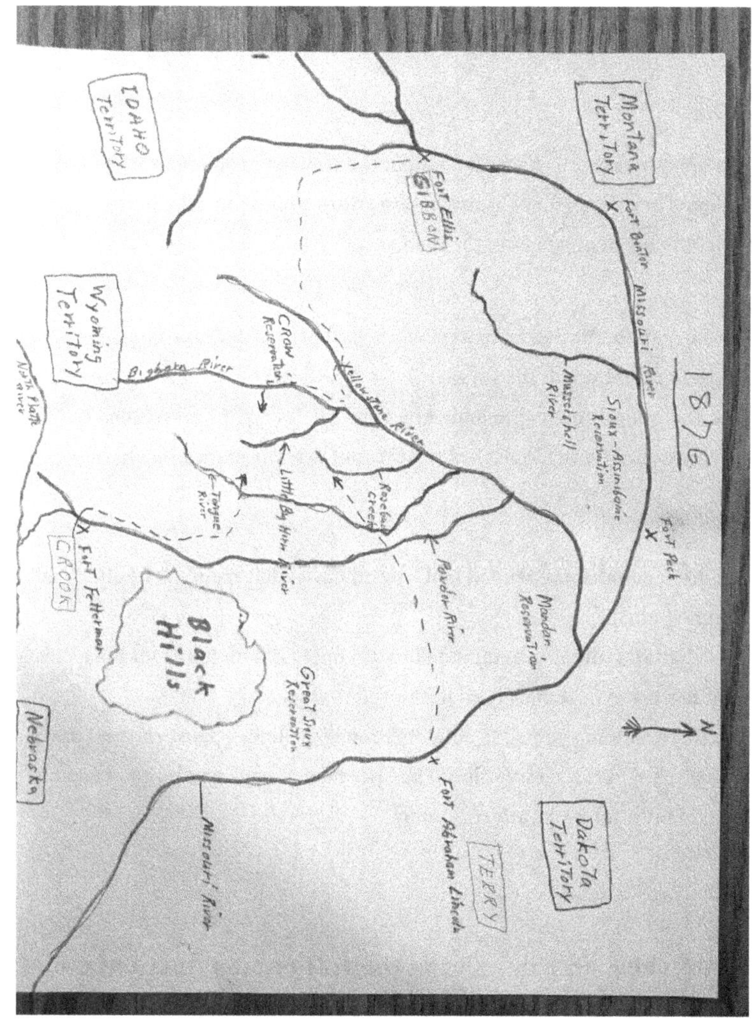

Colonel Custer commanded the 7th cavalry attached to General Terry coming from Fort Abraham Lincoln.

The army was more concerned about the Indians escaping as had happened before. They never thought the Indian tribes would put up a fierce fight. Not with this big of an army in the field.

Thus began the Indian campaign of 1876. Three different columns of soldiers set up to round up all the savages.
The Dakota column commanded by General Terry which included the 7th cavalry under Custer, marched west from Fort Abraham Lincoln.

Another column commanded by General Crook left from Fort Fetter-man and marched north.
The Montana column commanded by Colonel Gibbon left from Fort Ellis and went down the Bozeman Trail to the Yellowstone.
The three columns hoped to catch the renegade tribes between them and return them to the reservation. They planned to converge on the Indians traditional summer hunting grounds.

Meanwhile, on a derelict spacecraft named the Centennial Buzzard. Somewhere in outer space.

Tara, who is a humanoid android, is preparing Les Didlin, who is a dumbass human being (mostly) for another stint in the rejuvenator chamber aboard the spacecraft.

Les is mostly mortal so extended space ship travel through the cosmos: which takes an inordinate amount of time, would render him a dried up old prune before they arrived at their destination. Which is unknown because they escaped from Mars just in time. Both Tara and Les were scheduled to be returned to Earth and recycled into something useful. So they hijacked the Centinial Buzzard and blasted off for parts unknown. Anyway all this happened in the future and isn't important here.

(See LES DIDLIN DESPERADO if you are curious about this)

Not highly recommended by the American literary society who display inept fortitude for questionable novels

So Tara has put Les in a state of suspended animation which required shaving off his ridicules mustache, stripping him naked and plopping him into a vat of vinegar. Or dill pickle juice. Whichever was handy. *Actually it might have been fermented turnip juice which might explain some things.* This concoction would rejuvenate his body and restore it to youthful vigor so that he might enjoy centuries of floating around in deep space as a pickle. (Or sauerkraut) Well, something strange happened. Just as she dumped him into the pickle vat the space craft entered into a time warp vortex. Thunder roared, lightning flashed, a rainbow hued cyclone of antimatter engulfed them. And Pepto Bismo: they were transported through time and space, back to Earth to the American Frontier in the year 1876. Right smack dab into the Indian Wars.

TARA MAKES A GRAND APPEARANCE

Tara appeared out of a lightning bolt that struck the ground. Once the crackling stopped and the grass quit sizzling, the smoke cleared and there she was. Her spaceship casual form fitting leisure suit had turned sparkling white with streaks of rainbow beams splashed across the front and back. Some tiny electric sparks danced from her finger tips. Her entire body glowed.

She startled a group of Cheyenne and Sioux Indian chiefs who were holding a powwow while smoking peyote. These chiefs had been discussing the merits of going to war with the white soldiers who were bound to come looking for them since they had ignored the army's orders to get their red butts back to the reservation or face the consequences. However, by the time Tara made her dramatic appearance , the discussion had turned to prime horseflesh some nearby Shoshone Indians were in possession of and some primo females that also resided in some Shoshone lodges.

These Cheyenne and Sioux were encroaching on the Crow and Shoshone hunting grounds. They had no use for the Crow who were aligned with the whites and often served as scouts and guided white soldiers to Cheyenne villages.

So they hated the Crow. The Shoshone were aligned with the Crow. But in these Cheyenne chiefs opinions, Shoshone women were better looking than

Crows. And hot to trot if you believed rumors. The chiefs were thinking about making a raid to steal ponies and capture some delectable womenfolk. Then *KaBoom!* Tara appeared.

She is a very fine looking android. She is finer looking than the finest looking human female. Now with her grand entrance and sparkling appearance she was totally awesome. She had these Horney chiefs flummoxed. (Whatever the fuck that means.) These chiefs took her for a spirit goddess. One that liked to fool around they hoped. Alas, although having all the necessary equipment, Tara isn't a party girl. She had managed to keep Les at bay for years, although she has been slightly tempted to fool around on occasion.

She put these guys straight in no time. If they tried any hanky panky with her, she promised to make their dicks shrivel up and fall off. She demonstrated by jolting the nearest chief below the belt with a spark from her fingertip. The guys dick didn't exactly shrivel up. Instead it quivered and smoke came out of the end of it. That convinced most of them, especially smoking dick.

She ascertained they were native Americans so she asked them what they were doing here. They told her they were gathered to figure out how to deal with the encroaching whites who were kicking them out of the Black Hills.

Now the chiefs figured they had over a thousand warriors. Maybe two thousand if more bands kept showing up. Time to kick some white man butt.

Then she told them they were cruising for a bruising because the cavalry was coming. And the infantry too. The U.S. Army wouldn't stop until they were all back on reservations or dead.

They told her there was too many of them gathered here. They weren't afraid of a few troopers, most of whom couldn't hit a buffalo in the ass with a Spencer rifle at fifty yards. No white man would dare attack them.

She asked them if they ever knew of any smart white men. That got them to thinking. Maybe this woman born in a lightning bolt might be worth listening to. They scheduled another powwow the day after tomorrow. Right now they had more pressing issues, like stealing horses or women or keeping the women they already had happy.

Tara needed to convince these chiefs that the U.S. government was serious. The army wasn't going to stop until all of them were herded back to reservations.

Tara knows all this stuff because when Elon created her to accompany the first human that his supersized space ship took to Mars: he gave her a super advanced internal computer loaded with everything known to humankind up through the year 2019. She was an artificial intelligence super genius. She had kept up with all the new updates while on Mars so she was up to date.

Tara scrambled up to the top of the nearest hill. She attempted to contact Les. He had to be around here somewhere. Les might know what to do. Yeah right. Remember in previous episodes, Tara and Les are able to communicate

telegrapically, or is it telephonically, how about telepathically. Well, whatever, it was with their minds. With their minds, (*yep, no cell phone required, or hand signals*). From distances apart. Which came in handy in case someone was eves dropping or lip reading. Also remember that Les very seldom comes up with good ideas. The fact is Tara was created to protect him. Oh right, Les happens to be the first human that Elon Musk sent to Mars. But that is another totally implausible story.

Les apparently was incognito or otherwise occupied . Tara would try later.

Meanwhile Les makes his appearance

Les arrived at the tail end of a lightning storm. A thunderous lightning bolt drove him into the ground. That might have hurt but as luck would have it, the ground was sort of squishy. He came to lying in a muddy buffalo wallow. He was dazed and confused. He stood up and was amazed and dumbfounded. Then he discovered he was naked and alone. Not only that but his greenish colored skin and light brown hair were changed.

(You would know about that if you read LES DIDLIN DESPERADO). Apparently time warp travel turns green skin to copper tone and hair black.

Les thought he might look a lot like a native American Indian. Or a Mexican. Or maybe an India Indian Or a Spanish Vaquero. Or someone who spent way too much time in a tanning booth. He climbed up to the top of a nearby hill to look around.

Damn, this country looks familiar. Yep, he was definitely back on Earth and since Les was an amateur geologist/ geographer/historian/naturalist and bird watcher, he ascertained he was somewhere on the Northern Plains of North America, or the plains of eastern Ukraine or the Plains in Spain where the rain falls mainly.

Then he heard a Meadowlark sing.. Holy crap! I'm in Montana. Reasoning being that the Meadowlark is the state bird of Montana. And he had never heard of a Ukrainian meadowlark. Or a Spanish one.

He was congratulating himself on being so clever when something way off in the distance caught his eye. He ran that way to check it out. Thirty minutes and five miles later (Les is a pretty fair cross country runner, even barefoot,) he topped a rise and behold a small buffalo herd. That herd was within spitting distance. In fact one of them snorted and blew snot all over Les's face.

Then he heard the crack of a rifle. One buffalo dropped dead. Then another and another shot and more dead buffalo. Les zeroed in on the source of the gunfire. He spied five men kneeling on a small rise about a hundred yards down wind from the herd. Their buffalo rifles were supported on tripods to

aid in their accuracy. They had a wagon loaded with hides and a team of mules. Their horses were hidden in a draw behind them. (*Note, Les is blessed with extremely awesome eyesight. He can spot a pimple on a pigs ass fifty yards away. Not that he has actually been looking for pig's pimples.)*

Buffalo Hunters! The SCUM of the earth as far as Les was concerned. These bastards were killing all the bison for their hides and leaving the meat to rot. Which meant that the local plains Indians wouldn't find anything to eat at their only supermarket. Les meant to stop this carnage right here and now. He jumped up and down and yelled and ran at the herd waving his arms. The herd bolted. They run off licketity split. This perturbed those hunters. Les figured they had intended to shoot the whole herd. And those buffalo were making it easy just standing there. They apparently had never been shot at before. But apparently some crazy person had run at them waving his arms before and this spooked them.

Les ran for a half mile along with the herd until they veered to the left and took off down a ravine. He stopped to look back at the hunters. One took a pot shot at him but the slug hit the dirt in front of him. Really guys? You shooting at me just for scaring your buffalo away. Les hadn't figured on that response. Fortunately He was out of their range. Damn, those hunters seemed really perturbed. Then things took a change for the worse.

The hunters mounted up and came charging down at Les. They intended to fix him good for spooking their buffalo herd away.

Three of them took potshots at him as they rode closer. The bullets didn't even come close. It's difficult to hit something while riding full out on horseback. In fact, a 50 cal Sharps rifle has such a kick it's even hard to stay in the saddle. Les didn't worry about these three for now. They hung back to reload. It's hard as hell to reload a sharps rifle on the gallop. It takes a moment or two.

The other two came on and attempted to ride right over him and trample his ass. He jumped out of the way of the first one. Then he ducked out of the way when the next rider tried a close range shot. It missed.

Les grabbed a bridle as the horse raced past. He vaulted up on it's back and kicked the rider out of the saddle. Then he wheeled his horse around and charged straight at the three following riders. Their next shots went wide and he galloped past. One bullet whizzed past his ear. Les leaped out of the saddle and grabbed one of the passing riders off his horse and they both hit the ground.

That man rolled to his side and drew a revolver. Before he could shoot, Les heard another rifle crack and the man's chest exploded. Les jumped to his feet ready to fight but that distant rifle cracked three more times and three more men fell. The remaining man jerked his mount around and hi-tailed it. A lone rider came out of a small gully and chased after him.

It was a short chase. The lone rider rode a superior horse. A big pure white stallion. The lone rider caught the fleeing hunter and stuck a tomahawk in his back. He tumbled out of the saddle. The rider dismounted. Then did some

things to that buffalo hunter with a knife. Gruesome things. He wasn't getting back up ever again for sure. He probably would never make it to the happy hunting grounds without certain items of his anatomy either.

Les stood as his rescuer approached. It was a woman. With flaming red hair. She dismounted and looked him over. Les looked her over too, very closely. She was a stunner. She stood over six feet with well toned muscles and a beautiful all over dark suntan complexion. And she was as naked as he was. Except for a rawhide belt and a knife scabbard and a pouch for rifle cartridges.

She spoke a few words he didn't understand so she tried some English on him. Les mostly knows English.

"You aren't from around here are you. And you aren't a Sioux or a Cheyenne either."

"Nope. I'm not any kind of Indian that I know of."

"Good thing you aren't a Crow. I'd be inclined to scalp you. You gonna give me any trouble?"

"Nope."

She tossed him a knife. "Get busy. We need to skin and gut these buffalo before the flies get to them and they rot." She mounted her horse.

"Where you going?"

"Gotta catch the horses unless you can pack a few hundred hundred pounds of buffalo meat on your back. We'll talk later."

Okay fair enough. Les was pretty sure she didn't intend to gut and skin him too. At least not right away. He got to work.

She did stop and do some other gruesome things to those other dead buffalo hunters though. They wouldn't be using their genitals any more anyway.

Much later. It takes time to gut and skin seven buffalo and load the meat and hides on six saddle horses and two mules. She studied Les the whole time. Les felt she came to some sort of conclusion about him. She threw him a chunk of buffalo liver and indicated he should eat it. Okay, He could do that. The red haired woman led Les down to a little creek as he munched on the raw liver and began washing blood and grime off of them. Apparently she thought Les incapable of washing all of his extremities. Naturally Les developed a massive boner. Now he was concerned she might cut it off like she had done those buffalo hunters. He wondered if they got boners while they were dining. Probably not.

She smiled, appreciated at the results. Les took that as a good sign, especially since she wasn't holding a knife.

"I'm called Flaming Hair that Rides Hard."

"You can call me Red."

Les could understand the Flaming Hair bit but the Rides Hard mystified him.

"I'm Les Didlin."

"Really? Well, lets do something about that."

She threw him to the ground and jumped astride him and had her way with him. She didn't even need to threaten him with a knife. ***He's so easy.***

Later, Les figured what the Rides Hard part of her name meant. She went for seconds. Afterwards, Red figured that Les was misnamed about the Didlin part. The les part anyway.

They headed out afterward with the loaded horses and mules. All the mounts were loaded with meat and hides and the guns and ammo they had taken off the dead hunters, so they walked. Flaming Hair that Rides Hard told him about herself as they walked. They were headed for her village that was camped at the mouth of Rosebud Creek. She had been adopted by the Cheyenne when she came to this area several years ago. Now she was a Cheyenne warrior. She never wanted to go back. She explained why. The Cheyenne are the freest people on the planet. Made sense to Les.
"Where did you come from?" Les asked.
She looked him in the eye. "I'm a time traveler just like you. I saw you appear out of the lightning flash. That's how I arrived here too. I came from this area but it was from the future. I'm from 2019. Back there I was a deputy U.S. Marshal.
"No shit! " Les was almost ready to believe anything this wild woman told him but this flabbergasted him. He decided to test her story.
"What happened in 2019?"
"A Corona virus pandemic."
"When did humans land on Mars?"
"Stupid question, people haven't even gone back to the moon yet. What was that-about forty years ago."
Hmm, so far so good. Okay a final question.

"What year is it now?"

"It's June 22, 1876. I know because the equinox was yesterday."

"How do you know that."

"By watching and observing and eavesdropping on white traders conversations, and spending all my time outdoors studying mother nature and the stars; instead of watching TV or staring at a computer screen or a smart phone. All that shit is making modern humans dumbasses."

Les figured he ought to take a stab at showing he wasn't an ignoramus or a dumbass so he said. "The battle of the Little Big Horn happened on June 25, 1876."

"I knew it was sometime in June. My people are heading for the Little Big Horn. There's a powwow scheduled between the Cheyenne and Sioux and some other tribes. They want to talk about the whites taking the Black Hills away from us. I know what happens after they kick the 7th calvary's butt. I tried to convince them to head for the Missouri breaks instead. Lots of game there and nobody else wants the place. At least for a few more years. We could hide out up there. But they want to see what this big powwow is all about. I just hope I can keep them away from the fighting. They've seen too much of it already."

"You've been fighting with the calvary?"

"No, not yet at least. Our camp was attacked by a bunch of white men, probably prospectors and miners who wanted to drive us out of the Black Hills. The bastards discovered gold there."

They traveled a bit further while they sized each other up some more.

Les broke the silence. "What do you know about time travel. It's kind of a mystery to me."

"I think you have to be in a certain place at the right time and get randomly sucked up into some force field and presto, you get deposited somewhere else in a different time."

"So it's totally random."

"Far as I know. I wasn't looking to be transported here, it just happened."

"A mystery we may never solve, huh."

"Yep. So where are you from Les?"

"Oh boy, you won't believe this. I started out in Montana as a kid, tried to be a cowboy but the pay sucked, moved to Arizona, where I worked as a part time private investigator. Where the pay really sucked so I had to supplement my income by picking up dog poop. Then I got involved with some crazy people and then got sent to Mars by an evil genius named Elon. Tara and I lived there awhile. Then a bunch of other people and things came and the place turned to shit. Tara and I escaped on a spaceship because they were going to ship us back to earth and recycle us into something useful. Then we got caught up in some kind of time warp voodoo and here I am."

She looked skeptical.

"Hmm, that's okay Les, you really don't have to tell me. I wouldn't go around telling people I'm from Mars though. People might think you are touched in the head."

"So what or who is Tara."

"She is a very human life like android. Super smart. Practically indestructable. She was created to protect me for our trip to Mars."

That piqued Red's interest.
"Where is she now."
"I don't know. We got separated by the time warp."

They rode on until they came to a big river that was in flood stage.
"This is the Yellowstone. We cross here. My people are on the other side. I hope you can swim."
Red urged the horses and mules into the current. Les followed. Halfway across the water got deeper and the horses had to start swimming. The current swept them downstream a half mile to a sand bar. The rest of the crossing was easy. Only one horse drowned. It got spooked by a floating cottonwood tree and headed back the way they had come. It got pooped out and never made it.

They managed to keep the other horses headed in the right direction and climbed up a steep bunk to dry land.

They followed the south bank of the river for a couple miles.
Suddenly, Red held up her hand. She sniffed the air. "I smell Crow Indians. These crow scout for the army."
"How can you tell?"
"They stink like white soldiers. It's the rations they eat."
Les sniffed the air. Then he caught a whiff. "Wuff, it smells like bean farts."
"Yeah, that's from the army rations."

Whew. Les figured beans might affect Crow Indians worse than they did him. Those were some rank farts. Probably wet ones.

A bit later Red spotted the farting Crow army scouts across the river. She shouted a few obscenities at them. They shouted back. One started to cross. She shouldered her rifle and shot him in the head. She gave the rest of them the finger. The rest of the Crow high-tailed it up the opposite bank and disappeared.

"They won't try to cross the river now. They think I'm an evil spirit and that I just cursed the river. Crows are superstitious."

Les figured giving someone the finger in 1876 had a different meaning back then.

"You run into them before?"

"Yeah, they're scared of me. They have heard stories about how I was born in a lightning bolt and now protect the Cheyenne."

"What about the one who tried to cross."

"There's alway a few doubters."

June 23

The next morning they arrived at Flaming Hair who Rides Hard's camp. Les counted nine te-pees. There were four braves, three older than dirt, the other one so ancient looking he could have passed for a mummy. He saw a bunch of women and a whole passel of little kids milling about the camp. Wow he thought those old duffers really packed it to sire so many kids. Red set him straight. The oldest old fart was her adopted father and only half the women

and kids were his. Then She explained that the white men who drove them from the Black Hills killed many of the Cheyenne men who stayed behind to cover their escape. The whites were better armed with repeating Henry rifles and there were more of them.

Then Les noticed there were the dogs. Holy crap! Every kid must have two dogs at least. Les made a mental note to watch where he stepped.
Red sensed what Les was thinking. She said that the rest of the kids; teenagers, were further down the creek with the rest of the dogs. They were guarding the horse herd.
"How many horses?"
"Twenty last time I counted. We keep borrowing ponies from the Shoshone.
"How many dogs?"
"Only a dozen or so."
"How many teenagers?"
"Three boys and four girls. The other men are out hunting."

Red and Les entered the camp. Everyone was excited to see Red again. They were all really excited to see the horses and mules loaded with meat and hides. They had lost most of their provisions back in the Black Hills.
They were a bit skeptical of Les. He watched for any hostile signs.
Then he stepped in a big pile of dog shit. That cracked everyone up. Then the women started looking him over real close.

Les remembered he was still stark ass naked. So was Red but that didn't bother her. It bothered Les. He got a boner just thinking about her. Maybe that's why those women were so interested in hm. Oh cripes!

"I could use some clothes."

She led him to her te-pee. He followed. Damn, She had a fine looking ass. He got a bigger boner. Those women noticed. They gestured and chatted in Cheyenne. Red grabbed him and pulled him inside.

"Lets not let that go to waste." They didn't.

Much later they emerged from the te-pee and found the entire village gathered around them. This time the hunters had returned. Just six young men. They must be the studs of the village. But only six and only two had rifles. This camp would be easy picking for a company of calvary.

Red discussed some things with everyone, then she turned to Les.

She told him everyone welcomed him and that they had named him *Man who steps in dog shit.*

Les wasn't pleased. Then Red laughed and said she was joking. His new Cheyenne name was Runs With Buffalo. She had told them about how she found him scaring the animals away from the buffalo hunters. Les figured Runs with Buffalo was a heap sight better than Man who steps in Dog Shit. It was even better than Les Didlin. He liked these people.

BACK AT THE ENCAMPMENT ON THE LITTLE BIG HORN

Tara surveyed the huge Indian encampment spread out in the valley below her. It was truly impressive sight. Thousands of lodges. Sioux, Cheyenne,

Arapaho, with some Blackfoot and other bands were congregated here. If Custer could see this the coming events might never happen. But she knew he wouldn't until he was already committed and it would be too late. There was nothing she could do to prevent what had happened from happening. Especially since she had that mandate of *harm no human*. She just hoped that Les wasn't going to be sucked into the hostilities, if he was around here that is. That's when Sitting Bull rode up and dismounted.

He came for a chitchat.
"I hear from the other chiefs that you appeared from a lightning bolt and they believe you are a powerful spirit that can shoot lightning from your fingertips. They say you know of the future."
"Yeah, that's partly true. My circuits got overloaded from the lightning but that's passed. See, no more lightning from my fingers."
"Do you know of the future. I had a vision about blue soldiers falling like grasshoppers from the sky. I believe that it meant we will have a great victory."
"I know your future. You will have a great victory soon. But afterward more blue soldiers will come. They will chase you all summer and all fall and all winter until your people are starving. They will not stop until all your people are forced onto reservations."
"That is a disturbing future you foretell. Is there nothing I can do to change it?"
"No, there are too many white men who will move onto your hunting grounds. The Army will never stop pursuing your people. You will be forced to escape

into Canada with some of your people for a while but will have to return and surrender."

"Our way of life will end."

"Sadly, yes. You should make sure your children and their children remember the old ways. That is important or they will become lost."

"This is a sad time for me. What of your future?"

"I can't see it. I have a companion I seek. Perhaps you will meet him."

"Perhaps."

Sitting Bull mounted his horse and rode away.

Tara walked away. Maybe Les was closer to the Powder River. She headed east overland. Apparently their telepathic comms were disabled when they went through the time and space warp. She would have to find him physically.

LES LEAVES THE ROSEBUD

Red wanted to scout ahead of her people. They had packed up camp after processing the meat she had brought. They were still intent on joining the big powwow in the Little Big Horn Valley. She was sure no hostiles were between the Rosebud and the Little Big Horn so she wanted to check that no Crow scouts or bluecoats had crossed to their side of the Yellowstone.

Les went with her. She had loaned him her strawberry roan mare. It was kinda skittish and just green broke. They rode back to where the Rosebud emptied into the Yellowstone and then turned upstream. They followed the shoreline looking for tracks.

A few miles upstream they rounded a big sweeping bend in the river. The river channel was wider and the water level had dropped since they had crossed. That's when they saw new horse tracks in the mud coming up out of the river and going up the southern bank. Those were shod horses. The horseshoes made unmistakable impressions.

Calvary had crossed here! Red counted at least eight set of tracks. A small scouting patrol. They had to head them off before they ran smack dab into Red's people. She took off at a fast gallop. Les urged the roan after her but it was no match for her white stallion. Soon she was over a mile ahead of him.

He followed her down into a small valley. She topped the opposite ridge line just as he reached the bottom. She no sooner disappeared from view than a whole bunch of gunshots rang out. Les urged his horse faster. Halfway up the hill he met Red coming back down. She had a bunch of bluecoats chasing her. A bullet creased the roans neck and burned a furrow across Les's thigh. He tried to turn but his horse was spooked. It kept galloping straight at the troopers. He plowed into two of them and all three horses went down. The other troopers galloped past and then turned their mounts to come back and help their fallen comrades.

Les landed on his feet. His horse sprang up and headed down hill. Les tackled one trooper who was getting to his feet. The man was a skinny little

wiry runt and put up a spirited tussle. Les finally pinned him down. Les smashed his face into the ground which stunned the little bugger and then rolled away to keep from getting bashed in the head from the rifle butt the second trooper swung at him. Les saw this guy wore sergeants chevrons. That probably meant the guy could handle himself in a fight. He was a big bruiser too.

By now the rest of the troopers had wheeled around and were charging back up the hill toward him. Les ducked another wild swing of the sergeants rifle and closed in to plant a hard right to the guys gut, he followed with an elbow to the guys throat. That put him down on his knees gasping for breath. Les kicked him in the head. That laid the man out. Les had a split second to pick up the rifle. It was a single shot trap door Springfield. The other troopers were almost on him. He only had a second to pull a shell from the sergeant's bandoleer and load. He fired from the hip and shot the lead trooper in the chest. Then he rolled out of the way as the others tried to gallop right over him. One swung a saber at him but he blocked it with the rifle. Then a shot rang out.

It was Red's 50 cal. Sharps. She had turned around and was coming to his rescue. That trooper was blown plumb out of the saddle. Les dove to the ground to evade another trooper who took a slash at him. By now the milling horses had stirred up a thick dust cloud. Les crawled over to a downed trooper and took the man's colt revolver. Then that sneaky little runt that he had slammed into the ground shot him in the ass. Les spun around and shot

the little bastard in the head. That tough little shit flew backwards. He lost his revolver. Then he sat up and just shook his head. Then he caught a runaway horse and vaulted up into the saddle and galloped away. Les watched him go. Then another runaway mount barreled over him. Les forgot about that tough little runt. He found the revolver in the dirt and shot the saber out of another troopers hand. Lucky bastard, Les was aiming at the guys chest. Another trooper fired several shots from his revolver at him. One bullet creased his shoulder. He kept moving.

By now everything was chaos. Some horses were out of control, spooked by the smell of blood and gun smoke and shouting men. Les kept ducking and rolling and zigging and zagging. He fired off more quick shots which might have wounded some men. The troopers fired off a bunch of wild shots at Les but they only winged him a couple more times. The dust got really stirred up. Nobody saw Red coming.

Red didn't bother to reload. She galloped right into the swirling mass of troopers full speed. Her horse barreled into at least three calvary mounts and sent them ass over teakettle. She threw her tomahawk and hit a trooper in the chest. He fell out of the saddle, mortally wounded. Then she bailed off her horse and tackled another trooper who was trying to regain control of his mount. They went down in a tangle of arms and legs and assholes. She stuck her knife in his heart. She took his revolver and shot another one in the arm. That was the last live round in the gun. She threw it and hit another man in

the head. Then she picked up a lost saber and sliced a long gash in another troopers leg as he rode by.
By now only a couple troopers were't dead or wounded or cut or clobbered by something. That's about when the remaining troopers figured they were outclassed by the red haired she devil and got the hell out of there. A couple were riding double because their horses had skedattled. They left their dead behind. They left their unconscious sergeant too because he sure looked dead.

Red jumped on her white stallion and caught one of the runaway horses. She brought it back to Les. He was looking at his butt wound. Son of a gun that smarts. Fortunately Les has butt skin as tough as tree bark. The bullet was only an inch or so deep and Red popped it right out with the tip of her knife.

"We probably ought to get out of here Les. Those calvary boys will bring back reinforcements, more than the two of us can handle."
She told him she had spotted a big column of infantry a few miles away. The squad of calvary they just run off was probably the infantry's advance scouts.

Les recalled what history he knew about this campaign. "That must be Colonel Gibbons command coming from Fort Ellis. He had infantry and calvary totaling over 450 men. "
Something was screwy. If Les remembered his history correctly, Gibbons shouldn't be on this side of the Big Horn River. Not yet anyway. In fact Les was sure Gibbons even had trouble getting across to this side of the Yellowstone. If Red was right about the date then Gibbons was close enough

to rescue Custer. He probably had other Calvary patrols scouting out the Big Horn and Little Big Horn right now.

Red and Les agreed. They had to do something or a lot more Indians and soldiers were going to die tomorrow morning. Les had a plan. Red was skeptical but agreed to go along with it. They needed to slow up or distract Gibbons enough so he couldn't help Custer. If he got to the battle in time he just might keep Custer from getting wiped out. Or the combined Sioux and Cheyenne might wipe him out too. His 450 men would be up against twice that many well armed Indian warriors.

Les said,"I gotta do something first."

A few minutes later Les was all outfitted in the unconscious sergeants trousers and shirt. Red took the man's blue coat. She thought she looked like a real badass sergeant now. Les agreed. They left the sergeant in his long johns. He was still out cold.

They had borrowed all the dead troopers guns and ammo so they were well armed with two loaded revolvers each, and a Springfield carbine with a bandoleer of cartridges.

Les rode northwest toward the infantry Red had spotted. He planned to slow them down and hopefully lure them back toward the Yellowstone. He hadn't figured out how just yet.

Red rode southwest toward the Little Big Horn Valley. She hoped to alert the Indians about the approaching army. If she encountered any calvary or crow scouting parties she planned to lure them back north toward the Yellowstone. She had a pretty good idea how to lure calvary. They were just men after all.

What man wouldn't chase a naked Indian maiden? If that didn't work she would shoot a few. They would definitely chase her then.

Just before they split up she told Les. "If we don't meet back up across the Yellowstone in a day or two then you will find me in the Missouri Breaks." Les liked that plan. He was beginning to like living on the northern plains in 1876. He was really beginning to like Flaming Hair that Rides Hard's company too. She had never even called him a dumbass. Not even once. It sure beat living on Mars or on a space ship. Now if only he would run into Tara, this would be perfect. It sure wouldn't hurt to have a protector given all the scrapes he was getting into. And he really missed her too.

COLONEL CUSTER JUNE 24 -25 1876

Custer's scouts reported they had found a big Sioux camp located in the Little Big Horn Valley. He had been following (He hoped) a band of Sioux or Cheyenne down the Rosebud. Custer was afraid the Indians would escape. He moved his command across the divide and proceeded down Reno Creek. That night he outlined his plan. Benteen was to scout the area to the south in case the Sioux were escaping that way. Custer and Reno took their men down Reno Creek for a few miles. Then Custer took his men up over the ridge to go overland and get ahead of any Indians escaping down the Little Big Horn.

Reno proceeded down Reno Creek to the confluence of the Little Big Horn. There he formed his men into a line and headed down stream . Soon he encountered several hostiles. He ordered his men to a fast trot and soon saw the huge Sioux and Cheyenne camp. Over a thousand lodges, over seven thousand Indians with nearly 2000 warriors. He stopped and formed a skirmish line. The Indians attacked in force.

Meanwhile Benteen found no hostiles to the south so he rejoined the pack train and proceed to follow Reno.
By now Custer knew Reno was in trouble. Custer attempted to find a way down to the Little Big Horn to support Reno. He sent messages back to Benteen to hurry and bring the ammo packs.

Reno was forced to retreat. He formed another skirmish line in the woods along the river bank but his force was too small to hold the position. Then the Indians started the woods on fire. He ordered another retreat to cross the river and go to the high ground on the other side. This turned into a rout and he lost at least a third of his men.

By this time Custer had split his command again and sent one company down to the Indian camp to draw off some of the braves attacking Reno. They were met by an overwhelming number of warriors and they were driven back. He left another company on a ridge as a rear guard. Indian warriors poured up the ravines from the river. Both companies were overrun. Custer took his remaining companies down to the river and temporally stopped the Indians

advance. But more and more warriors joined the battle and drove him back. He left one company to cover his withdrawal. They were promptly overrun.

Reno formed a strong fighting position atop his bluff and held off the Indians. Many of the warriors left that engagement to join the battle against Custer. Custer probably realized he was in deep shit now but his companies were scattered in a number of positions. Some surviving members of Custer's immediate command retreated to a hilltop. There they shot their horses to use as breastworks. This is where they made their last stand. Soon they were all overrun.

Benteen joined up with what remained of Reno's force and they held off further attacks on their position the rest of the day and night.
Indian sharpshooters harassed them most of the next day while the huge Indian camp dispersed. The Battle of the Little Big Horn was over.

Previously, before Reno commenced his attack.

Red ran into another calvary patrol a couple hours after she left Les. She rode right at them. They were confused by the blue coat she wore. Was she a crow scout from General Ellis. They let her ride right up to them. She kicked her horse into a full gallup then and rode right through the startled troopers. She fired her revolvers at them until they were empty. The troopers reacted too slow to return fire until she was clear. Then she rode low and fast and

dodged around some rocky outcrops. None of their shots hit her and she rode out of range. She had put bullets into six men. Two were fatal shots. That left six uninjured troopers. Four of them chased after her. The rest limped back to the main column.

Red circled around and headed northeast back toward the Yellowstone. The troopers chased until they lost her trail. They returned to the army column and reported that she was heading to the Yellowstone. Was she heading for the suspected Indian camp? Gibbons called his officers together. Should they go after her and maybe find the main Indian encampment?

About that time Les rode into view. They mistook him for a trooper from General Ellis's Column. He rode in all excited and told a tall tale about Ellis finding the big Indian camp and attacking but he was in trouble because the Indians outnumbered his force. He needed help fast. Before this info sunk in, Les grabbed a fresh mount and took off toward the Yellowstone. He yelled FOLLOW ME as he galloped away. Ellis ordered a company of calvary to go after him. Then he ordered his entire column to follow.

The troopers chasing Les weren't completely sure who he appeared to be. That was strange, him taking a fresh mount and riding out before anyone could question him. He really didn't look like a trooper either. He looked more like an Indian. But he didn't look like any of the Indian scouts they had seen. They followed him most of that day. He always kept a good half mile ahead of them. Every so often he stopped and waved them on. Dusk approached. The troopers decided to turn back.

Les saw them turn around. He didn't want them to. Not yet. So he rode back and when he got close enough he drew his revolvers and opened fire. His bullets hit the ground mostly in front of the troopers but sure got their attention. He hoped to piss these guys off enough to chase him. When he ran out of bullets he shot them the middle finger. These guys knew what that meant. He had screwed them over. That worked, probably too good. They had a couple sharpshooters who dismounted and took careful aim and shot his horse out from under him.

Les took off running. He runs pretty fast. But just a bit slower than a fatigued horse. Those troopers gained on him. Fortunately he was only a mile from the river. They almost caught him. He slid down a steep bank while bullets kicked up dirt all around him. He plunged into the Yellowstone just twenty yards ahead of them. They took potshots from the bank as he swam toward the opposite side. Then he went under. The current took him downstream.

Les can hold his breath an inordinate amount of time, especially if someone with a rifle is waiting to shoot him in the head when he came up for air. He stayed under. The current carried him away. The troopers decided he was a goner. They made camp and waited for the main column to catch up.

Meanwhile Gibbons's Crow scouts caught up to him. They told him they had discovered the huge Sioux/Cheyenne camp back in the Little Big Horn Valley. He turned his men around but it was getting dark so they made camp for the

night. Les and Red had delayed them long enough. They wouldn't get to the Little Big Horn in time to rescue Custer.

Their approach however, might have convinced the Indians to break off contact with Reno and Benteen. The huge Indian camp moved out. Some headed for the Bighorn mountains. Some headed back east toward the Rosebud. A few headed north. Nobody headed south. General Crook was that way.

BACK ON THE YELLOWSTONE

Les managed to crawl ashore a couple miles further downstream. It was totally dark. He was bone tired. He was hypothermic from the icy cold water. He had a nasty head wound and a couple other bullets had grazed his arms and another one had plowed into his butt cheeks. Damn, why was he always getting shot in the butt?? He dragged himself up onto a sand bar and zonked out. He had washed ashore still on the south side of the Yellowstone.

A little after dawn someone kicked him awake. It was that sergeant they had stolen the clothes off of. Time for round two.

Les caught the troopers foot as he tried to kick him again. He pulled the trooper down and they rolled around, punching and biting and pulling hair. The sergeant was highly motivated. Les was wounded and plum tuckered out. He got kneed in the balls. Socked in the mouth. Bitten on the arm, scratched

across his face and punched in the stomach. The sergeant pulled his hair, pushed his face into the dirt, slammed his head repeatedly into a big rock, kicked him in the butt and generally beat the shit out of Les.

The sergeant finally stopped to catch his breath. Then he made a mistake. He called Les a dumbass.

What! That roused Les from the near dead. Nothing pisses Les off more than being called a dumbass. He got to his feet and charged into that sergeant. He punched him in the face. Kneed him in the balls. Poked fingers in his eyes, bit an ear off, elbowed him in the neck and almost put the guy down with a roundhouse kick to the stomach. Les collapsed next to his opponent. The sergeant staggered over and grabbed Les by the hair and pounded his head on a rock a couple times. Then he sank to his knees. They were both too pooped to move.

Somebody walked up. "You boys through having fun yet?"

It was Tara! She helped Les to his feet. She told that sergeant he better stay down or she was going to cut his balls off. He stayed down.

"Come on Les, we need to get out of here. General Terry's army is only a couple miles away." Tara half pulled and half carried Les up the river bank and they disappeared into the hills.

"What did you do to that guy anyway?"

"Stole his pants."

"You should have given them back. They're filthy. What did he do to you?"

"Called me a dumbass."

"He was kicking your butt."

"No way, I had him right where I wanted him."

"Unhuh, You wanted him smacking your head against a rock."

They walked a couple miles.

Les had a throbbing headache. That damn rock. It was a bit harder than his head. He felt a little dent in his titanium skull. He thought about going back and kicking that sergeant in the nuts. Then he thought better of it. The bastard probably had found another rock by now.

"I'm glad you found me."

"Yeah, you need all the help I can give you. Where to now?

"I need to meet someone in the Missouri Breaks. She's a time traveler like us."

Les proceeded to tell Tara all about Flaming Hair that Rides Hard.

Tara said, "Oh shit. Elon warned me about her."

"That doesn't sound good. What's the story Tara?"

"Her real name is Sara. She was created before me. We were named alphabetically."

"Theres more of you?"

"Probably. Most were inferior and were destroyed. Sara was perfect. Too perfect it turned out. She doesn't have that mandate—*harm no human.* She also was sexually promiscuous. Sara escaped before Elon made corrections. In fact she escaped during a severe lightning storm. Maybe that's how. Maybe she got sucked into a time and space warp back then. No wonder nobody could find her. She lied to you about being a deputy U.S. Marshal. The Marshalls were actually looking for her."

"I guess that's why you don't fool around with men."
"Yeah, Elon decided that led to too many complications. He left me totally clueless as you know.
"Fucking Elon. he's the dumbass."
"Yeah he might be an evil genius."
Despite the new revelation, Les and Tara headed north toward the Missouri Breaks. It was as good a direction as any. Tara suspected something might be drawing Sara there. Maybe she had found a time warp portal there that enabled her to travel back and forth in time.

MEANWHILE RED STAYS BUSY

AFTER Red let the troopers astray she circled back and headed toward the Little Big Horn Valley. She reached the river in the dark where she stopped to water and rest her stallion. A couple hours before dawn she rode out. Red reached the Sioux pony herd before dawn. Then she rode into the outer camp and raised the alarm. She rode through the entire camp until she was at the furthest end. Warriors caught their ponies and grabbed their weapons and joined her there. Dawn arrived and right on schedule, Major Reno and his 120 or so men charged out of the trees.

Red led the Indian charge toward Reno. When he retreated she was right on his ass. When he regrouped in the tress she started the woods on fire. When he retreated across the river she turned and raced back to the main camp.

She rallied more warriors who had gathered their horses and weapons. Then she was in the lead as the Indians charged up a ravine and engaged Custer's scattered calvary companies. She was everywhere, riding her white stallion while cutting down straggling troopers. She had ditched the blue sergeants coat back at the river. The Sioux and Cheyenne were encouraged by this wild red haired naked woman warrior. They made quick work of Custer and his men.

When it was over Red galloped away. She didn't stop to strip the soldiers or to celebrate the victory. The Sioux and Cheyenne warriors never saw her again. Red went searching for her band but they had already headed west toward the Big Horn mountains. They had joined another larger band. She let them go.

Red knew the rest of the history of the Indian war of 1876. She had done all she could but history is real hard to change significantly. The freedom of these native Americans was coming to an end.

It was time for her to move on. She headed north toward the Missouri Breaks. Maybe she would find Les again. Maybe she would meet up with Tara. They had a lot in common. That might be interesting. Maybe she would get sucked into another time warp vortex and get transported to yet another era. This wasn't her first rodeo.

The sun set over the Northern Plains. A meadowlark sang its tune.

June 26, 1876 ended.

July 1, 1876

Flaming Hair that Rides Hard saw the storm coming. She was riding her stallion heading for the Missouri River. It caught her out in the open. This wasn't a normal summer thunder and lightning storm. It was something fierce. She realized what was coming. *Here we go again.* She was swept up in a swirling vortex and disappeared. Destined to alight somewhere someplace in another time.

Les and Tara were miles away. The same storm approached. They tried to take shelter in a stand of cottonwoods in a creek bottom. The wind hit like a cyclone. Huge thunderbolts crashed across the sky. Tremendous lightning bolts hit all around them. The air crackled with electricity.

Tara suspected this might happen. She had consulted her onboard wikipedia information banks and learned everything known about time warps back in 2019. She learned they required tremendous energy (lightning bolts would do) and some sort of catalyst. Warps or wormholes in the fabric of the universe existed in deep space and might be associated with the energy from a black hole. But why here on the earth's surface?

Then she realized, they were being sought out due to their own energy fields.

THE TIME WARP WAS SEEKING THEM!

She grabbed LES.

"HOLD TIGHT LES!"

THEY WERE SUCKED UP INTO A SWIRLING VORTEX.

Somewhere, sometime, they were destined to be deposited into yet another time. Their journeys had just begun. *Probably*.

The end of this episode

Great Plains Indian Lands before 1876

PRESENT DAY RESERVATIONS ON NORTHERN PLAINS

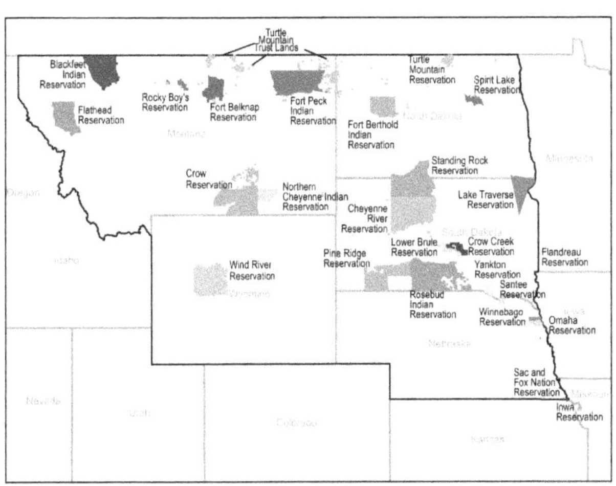

DATE AND LOCATION— UNDETERMINED

Here we go again

That storm which caught Les and Tara was, *yep you guessed it*; another portal through time and probably space. They held on tight to each other. A swirling lightning bolt filled cyclone of antimatter eventually deposited them on a flat plain.

The dust cleared. Static electricity crackled around them. Then all became quiet. They looked around. The air was choked with fine yellow dust. A slight breeze kept stirring it back up into the air. The ground was hard and flat and stretched out for as far as they could see. Which was about fifty yards. Tara switched to her infrared vision, the hard flat surface continued to the horizon. She switched to x-ray. "
This surface is several feet thick. It's like concrete." She stomped on it. "I think it's caliche. Natural occurring stuff made when calcium carbonate percolates through the ground. We might be on an ancient sea floor."
She tried her radar. Something in the distance moved toward them.

"Where the hell are we?"
"No idea. This doesn't compute with any known quantity.
Get down low Les. Something is coming toward us."
They hunkered down. Lightning continued to flash all around them. Thick dust settled all over them and stuck. "It's the static electricity attracting dust

particles. Don't move Les. My radar shows three objects approaching. They appear to be carrying something."

They waited, motionless. Minutes passed. The objects came into view.
Les held his breath. Tara didn't need to. Humanoids don't need to breathe. Lucky them because everything smelled horrible. Something like a mixture of rotting eggs and skunk with a dash of cat shit. The three objects materialized out of the yellow haze.
Les whispered "Are those people. Man they are ugly as shit."
"Shh, they are armed."
Les was right. These might be the ugliest people imaginable, if they really were people. They were tall, over seven feet and skinny as rails. Giant foreheads, enormous red eyes, sunken chests and pot bellies. Somehow the dust didn't stick to them. Tara was right. All three carried what looked like sniper rifles with big telescopic sights. The lead one held some kind of sensor in front of him. It swept the device back and forth as it walked. They walked right past Tara and Les and kept going.
Les slowly let out his breath. He'd been holding it for about seven minutes. The three things stopped and swirled around and pointed their weapons toward Les. He stopped breathing again. One fired at where it thought Les was. It missed him by a whisker. Les froze.

The three human like/things walked closer, sweeping their weapons from side to side. When they were almost upon her, Tara sprang up and grabbed the rifle away from one of the things and clobbered it in the chest with it. It flew

backward several yards. Les tackled the second one and pinned it to the ground. It thrashed around and tried to grab him by the hair so he punched it in the face. That made a squishy sound. The third one fired a burst of something that caught Tara in the back. She crumpled to the ground. Les jumped the third one before it fired again. He wrestled the weapon away and used it to jab the thing in its pot belly. That put it on the ground. Les stomped it's head in. He turned just in time to duck a shot fired from a side arm from the thing he had punched in the face. Tara swung her leg out and swept that one off it's feet. Les grabbed a rifle and smashed that one in the head. The head exploded like an eggshell. Then he stomped all three until they were flat. Squashed flat. Wherever they were, he was strong as heck. He stomped the shit out of those potbellies. Literally, because brown slime gushed out of their buttholes or whatever these things had for buttholes. These things were really fragile.

Tara sat up. She checked her vitals.
"How bad is it."
"My energy banks are shot. I've got about four hours of reserve power then I'll shut down."
"Anything I can do?"
"Yes, bring me those rifles and that gizmo the lead one was carrying. I might salvage parts from them that you can use to fix me temporally.

Tara got to work. Les examined the three corpuses. They had two arms, two legs, one head and the rest of them looked less and less humanoid. They had

narrow shoulders, sunken chests, pot bellies, long thin noses, an almost non-existent chin, no teeth, no hair, weak spindly arms and legs. The large forehead and big eyes made him think of alien mockups he had seen on earth. They were real creepy looking. These things wore silvery coveralls and sturdy boots and carried small backpacks. The packs held several containers of some brown slime and a couple metallic cylinders that must be power refills for their weapons. Tara figured the brown slime was food rations for the tall skinny creeps. Les figured he would rather starve than eat that stuff. He opened a container and took a whiff and promptly gagged. Oh my god ! The stuff smelled worse than the air they were breathing. He turned his attention to the rifles. The rifles fired electric charges, lightning bolts! Les handed the cylinders to Tara.

"Yeah, these will work as my emergency power, wire them in to my circuits and we are good to go."

Later.

"What now?"

"We get the fuck outta here. I think I'm good for a couple days so lets make tracks before more skinny creeps show up."

"Which way?"

"Lets see where they came from."

Tara did some calculating as they moved. Fortunately her memory banks and chronometer were undamaged. She did some calculations based on the maximum speed limit in the universe. (Einstein figured the speed of light was

as fast as anything could go which is 186,282 miles per hour. Which sounds pretty fast but consider this: the sun is 93 million miles away from earth or 8 light seconds. Distant stars happen to be several light years away.) Okay enough physics for now. Tara calculated that it took them 397 light minutes to be transported from their space ship back to Earth when they were sent back to 1876. Which means they were a very long way away. Probably near the edge of the solar system. (*Okay my math probably sucks but feel free to figure it out yourself. My calculation shows 2.76908e11, whatever the hell that means)*

***But* this time, the trip from 1876 to wherever they were now took just 100,000th of a light second. (*I hazard to guess that works out to 116.25 miles but who's counting?)* Which meant they didn't travel very far distance wise. Which meant they were still somewhere on Earth. But where? It sure as hell didn't look like Montana.**

Les asked if they were somewhere in the future. Tara explained that was impossible since they couldn't go somewhere in time before they had already experienced that time. (Some more mind numbing physics us mortals will never comprehend. Simply put, backward was the only option. You can't go somewhere you never been before by skipping ahead in time . *Beats me who figured that out*). Therefore she figured they had traveled back in time. Way way back before anybody knew much about before Earth as we know it existed.

"So we are in the past!"

"Yeah, the way way distant past."

This was beginning to get spooky. Then it got spookier. They walked a couple hours then suddenly a large shape materialized out of the dust haze. It was nearly ten feet long and about a foot high and was moving fast on six spiky legs. Suddenly the thing sensed them. It reared up and wings unfurled from its back. Then it flew right at them. Les was ready. He had confiscated one of the skinny creeps rifles but hadn't figured out how to operate it yet. So he swung it like a club and smacked the flying thing out of the air. Probably not a good idea because it jumped up and attacked him with the claws on its feet. Les smacked it down a few times but the damn thing kept getting back up and going for him again.

Clubbing it wasn't working. Les was pooping out. He had a hard time sucking in enough foul dusty air to keep fighting. The thing made another jump at him and knocked him flat. No way could Les protect himself against all six legs slashing at him with claws. He has pretty tough skin but not tough enough to keep from getting slashed open on his arms and legs. Tara jumped on its back and tried to stab it with the knife she always carried strapped to her thigh. No good, the things back was armor plated. It flapped it's wings which threw her clear. Les used that opportunity while Tara had distracted the thing to get his boot knife out. He had borrowed the boots from that calvary sergeant he stole the clothes from. Sara, or rather Red had given him the knife. He plunged it into the things underbelly. No armor there. Gobs of brown jelly like gunk poured out. Les ripped the things belly open clear to it's

asshole. That did it in. Les rolled clear. He was covered in the brown jelly crap. It positively reeked.

Tara examined the thing. Then she examined Les. Then she said. "Nice going dumbass. Next time try cutting the head off. That might save you from a shit bath.

They learned some things from the encounter. First was the guns were worthless because apparently only tall skinny creeps could fire them. Second was those skinny creeps probably were not soldiers searching for them but hunters looking for these winged armored creatures. Third , the brown slime was what the skinny creeps ate. *Eww ick!* Fourth, this creature sure resembled a giant cockroach and it apparently survived out here somehow so there must be some sort of food source for it. As far as Les and Tara knew, cockroaches can eat almost anything but not yellow dirt or concrete.

Tara made another observation. The cylinder power tubes they took from the skinny creeps packs were batteries. Lithium batteries. And the yellow dust that surrounded them was in fact lithium. Les said that's swell for you Tara, you can make a better more permanent power source but I need to occasionally eat real human kind of food and I'm not eating brown cock roach slime. And I need to drink something pretty damn soon cause I'm about parched. Tara said Les was acting like a dumbass again. They would need to find some kind of laboratory or machine shop to make a permanent battery for her. Did he see one of those anywhere.

They started walking again. Les kept a watchful eye out for more cockroaches. And a workshop hopefully. And a water well. Or a pool of stagnate filthy water. He was getting real thirsty. Tara fiddled with the gun she had kept. She was a smart android, sooner or later she would figure out how to operate it.

Eventually they came to a sheer wall. It was solid, and about ten feet thick and appeared metallic, something had definitely built it. It rose over thirty feet high. Was it there to keep things out or was it built to keep things in?

There was something else that puzzled Les ever since they arrived here, where ever they were. He felt lighter. Moved easier and a bit faster. Tara felt the same way. So when they decided to see what was over the wall, both jumped over fairly easily. Well Tara did. *She's such a show off.* Les took two tries before grabbing on to the top edge and pulling himself over. The gravity here is less that we are used to on Earth. We aren't on Earth or earth is smaller in this time. *Another puzzle for Tara to figure out.* Everything looks pretty much the same on the other side of the wall. They kept walking. Everything wasn't exactly the same though. Tara noticed it almost immediately. The surface was softer here, almost spongy like they were walking on top of arctic tundra that was thawing out. The air was a bit clearer too. Less dust for the wind to pick up.

A tall tower came into view. It was so tall it disappeared into the dust clouds overhead It was unmanned. Yep, no tall skinny creeps were around. No giant cockroaches waiting in ambush. A hidden door slid open as they

approached. It was a really thick door. More like a blast door that might stop an artillery round.

So the creeps knew about motion detectors. And maybe big artillery rounds. What else did they know. Tara and Les entered. Immediately some sort of vacuum static neutralizer automatically took all the dust off of them. It even took all the brown slime off of Les. The outside door closed.

Then another hidden door slid open. They entered a small room. The door closed. They were rocketed upward.

"Holy shit, this must be a supersonic elevator."

Les was practically plastered to the floor. Tara wasn't. She had noticed a harness apparatus as soon as they entered and managed to strap herself in just as the door closed. A couple seconds later the elevator stopped. The door slid open and they were greeted by six tall skinny creeps pointing rifles at them.

Les sat up. The creeps didn't blast him. He took that as a good sign. He got to his feet. Nobody blasted him. Another good sign. So he tried communication.

"Howdy doody assholes. Anybody got some water. I'm about parched."

The creeps stepped back. They looked at each other. They appeared to talk among themselves, hard to tell since they didn't actually speak out load but more like reading each others minds. Apparently they came to a unanimous decision. All six raised their weapons.

Les said, "Oh shit!" He dropped to the floor and rolled to the edge of the elevator. A lightning blast nearly got him, two more blasts hit the wall behind

him. Then the room was filled with lightning arcs. Electricity crackled. The room filled with a scorched pig shit smell and a putrid cloud of brown gunk. Les stayed still. The air cleared. Tara lowered her gun. All six of the skinny creeps were blasted apart. Hunks of them coated everything behind them.

"I got this stupid gun to work Les."

"No shit."

They looked around. They were in a very large room. It appeared to be made of glass windows because what wasn't smeared with scorched hunks of skinny creeps was transparent. They looked out. This room was so high up it was over the yellow dust cloud down on the planets surface. Tara scanned the horizon with her telescopic vision. She spied other towers in the far distance. She figured the closest was over fifty miles away. Les looked up. Now this was really strange. A large moon or planet covered about a quarter of the sky. Tara said now that explains everything. Les said HUH?

Tara explained one theory about the earths formation was that it collided with another planet. That planet was called THEIA. It was about the size of Mars. The accepted theory is that Theia collided with Earth head on about 4.5 billion years ago. The collision was so fierce the planets fused together. Earth got the better deal and ended up a bigger planet. Some of the debris from the collision was ejected and formed the present day moon.

"Wow, we really did go way way back in time."

"Yeah, no shit Les. Now we need to figure out a way to leave. Theia looks awfully close. We might be here for the collision. Meanwhile I suspect we will be getting some unfriendly company from those other towers real soon."

"Lets see what the creeps have here."

They searched the tower. It was about a hundred feet in diameter with the clear glass all around the outside wall. The interior was divided into various room, all with hidden doors. Some of which refused to open . Some did. They found a workshop. Tara set about repairing herself. Les went looking for something to drink. First he blasted the elevator door so it wouldn't work. *No creeps are getting up here on that elevator now.* Tara thought about calling him a dumbass again. Then she resigned herself to tolerating him. He was never going to change.

After exploring a bit more Les realized he had destroyed the only way they had to leave the tower. Yep, no stairways, no backup elevator. *Well fuck me, at least there wasn't dog shit to step in.* So far at least.

Tara noticed something weird going on outside as she worked. The sun began to set. The other planet began it's journey across the sky, the wind picked up so much that the tower shook and a severe lightning storm brewed down below. Then she saw what looked like dark rain clouds form all across the horizon. Rain fell in torrents. It washed the yellow dust out of the air and then a gigantic flash flood appeared. It covered all the ground surface she could see. It washed against the tower. Muddy water even splashed on the tower's top floor windows. Tara realized the water was being pulled along like a tidal wave caused by the gravitational pull of the other planet. Whoever built that wall did it to contain the flood water so it would eventually percolate down into the ground. The tall skinny creeps must need water! They had devised a wall to contain it and save it underground.

About that time, Les discovered a concealed shaft. It housed pipes and wires and cables that brought power and WATER up from somewhere underground. He followed a pipe to another well concealed thing that resembled a spigot. Oh yea, it was a water spigot. He waved his hand over it and Cool clear water came out. Les soaked it in. Then he called Tara.
"Hey guess what? I found a way out of here, I think. There's a shaft heading down full of pipes and shit. I'm checking it out."
Les grabbed a pipe and began sliding down. He was about 50 feet down when he realized something. Oh fuck! I'm not going to be able to climb back up, the pipes are too smooth and slippery. *Man what a dumbass.*

Meanwhile Tara finished her repairs. Then she studied the near planet. Was it getting bigger. We might be running out of time sooner than she had originally thought. She scanned the ground below. The air was temporally clear and she could see the other towers easily. Nothing stirred down below. Maybe the tall skinny creeps didn't get along with their neighbors. Maybe there weren't any neighbors. She scanned the horizon again with her telescopic vision. Something way out there caught her eye. Was that a spaceport? It was built up on a high platform. High enough to escape the flood. She saw huge cranes and perhaps launch towers. *We need to check that out.*
"Hey Les, I'm coming down."
The further Les slid down the pipe the slicker it got from condensation or maybe perspiration. He slid faster, then faster. He clamped his hands tighter on the pipe. He wrapped his arms and legs around it. He tried to jam his feet

again the shaft wall. It was slick and smooth too. He slid right past the ground level. Most of the pipes and cables and wires branched off. But not the one he was holding on to. That pipe kept going down. He kept sliding down. A long long way. He met the stench. This was even worse than all the stuff he had been smelling before. The stench even burned his eyes. He clamped them shut. Then he hit bottom.

Surprise! It wasn't hard concrete or rock or mud. Nope, he splashed into some kind of liquid. Deep liquid. He swam back to the surface. He opened his eyes. Apparently he had passed through the stench zone. What he was treading in was Thicker than water. Slimy too. Smelly too. Really smelly but not eyeball burning. Reminded Les of an open cess pool. *Oh fuck, I'm in creep shit.* Those bastards must have been dumping their crap down this shaft for years. For some reason the place was well lit. Bright in fact. The brightest shit hole he had ever been in. He looked up just in time to see Tara hurtling down at him. She plowed into him and they both went under. This time Les was driven deeper. This time he kept his eyes open. This time he realized the shit was thinner the deeper he got. How about that, creep shit floats!

Tara grabbed his arm. She pulled him toward an underwater passageway. They swam through and into another well lit chamber and then kicked for the surface. There was a platform and they hauled themselves out. The smell wasn't as bad here.

"Where the hell are we now?"

“I think we are deep in the bowels of a septic system. That first chamber was for floating shit. This one took the cleaner liquid near the bottom. It’s like a settling pond only in reverse. The bright lighting is zapping the stink out of the shit and dissolving the turds and then the finer stuff settles to the bottom and is sucked into this second chamber,” Leave it to Tara to figure out the plumbing system so quickly.

She continued. “See that pump over there? It’s pushing the cleaner clearer stuff back up to the top of the tower. I think the creeps drink that stuff.”

Les spewed vomit all over. “Ick, I drank that stuff.”

“How did it taste?”

“Hmm, well it was cool and it didn’t stink and it didn’t taste like shit.”

“Yeah, it probably goes through some filters on the way up.”

“I hope so.”

“Speaking of up, there’s a ladder over there. Come on Les. That’s our way to the surface.” And it was.

The ladder took them to the ground level where they found a doorway that led outside. Tara took the lead. They headed toward the possible spaceport she had seen. Darkness fell. Only it wasn’t total dark because static electricity crackled all around them. This was a really weird place. Tara set a fast pace. They reached their destination just as dawn broke over the horizon. Then the sun came up and turned everything so dazzling bright it hurt their eyes. That only lasted a few minutes though because Theia rose and slowly blocked out the sun. They were left with a corona of red and yellow light shining around

the planets edges. An eclipse. Theia looked even larger than it did last evening.

By the time they found a way up on top of the spaceport platform everything was blocked out by the yellow dust haze that settled around them. A wind came up. The dust got thicker. Tara led them into a large hanger like building. Nothing stirred inside. It was deathly quiet. The floor was strewn by yellow dust covered lumps. Long skinny ones. Les dusted some off. The lumps were dead creeps. The place looked like a massacre site. Tara looked around. She led Les outside.

"They weren't massacred Les. They committed mass suicide. "

"Why?"

"Because the last space ships left them behind. Everyone that could go left. Theia and Earth are going to collide and everything here will be destroyed. It's happening really soon."

"We are screwed then."

"Yeah, unless we find a time portal."

"Good luck with that. Those things just seem to find us whenever they please."

The words were barely out of Les's mouth when a massive lightning storm moved in. Bolts of supercharged energy hit all around them. A cyclone tornado hurricane wind (take your pick) cleared all the dust out of the air. The whole sky was filled with Theia, the planet was so close Les felt he could reach out and touch it. A swirling mass of blue and purple and crimson orange and palo verde green antimatter approached. The color doesn't matter because it was anti color, which is a bit like Technicolor on

Kodachrome at sunrise. Silver and gold sparkles shot out of the swirling mass. Les thought it looked pretty darn neat. Almost as neat as the planet looming over them that was fixing to obliterate everything.

"Hang on Les. Our ride is coming."

Just in time too because twelve hours later the planets collided. Preceded by a radiation loaded super wind that blew everything flat and cooked anything cookable.

IS THIS THE END?

Sorry folks but we may be just getting started. It's a big cosmos after all.

Onward and upward and then ring around the rosy with a splish splash.

Our time rovers fell out of the sky. Fortunately they had moved well beyond 4.5 billion years ago and some distance from the tall skinny creeps domain which no longer remained anywhere anyplace. Although it's possible some creeps inhabit roaming space ships endlessly seeking a suitable place to crash

land. But enough about them. They are nasty creatures that eat cockroach shit and pave over everything with concrete.

But back to Les and Tara.

Les surfaced sputtering sea water. He took a big gulp. Yeah, that's the real stuff. If memory serves you may recall that Les can occasionally drink seawater with no ill consequences except getting salt blisters on the end of his dick.

Tara surfaced beside him.

"Hey dipshit, take it easy on that stuff. Remember what happened last time you drank too much seawater."

Les quit gulping water. Salt blisters make a lasting impression. Oh and what's this. She called me dipshit instead of dumbass. Progress I think.

Tara consulted her autorotator gyroscopic time and location plausiometer. Yeah she is full of surprises. She determined they were in the middle of the Pacific Ocean on planet Earth in the year 1520. After a bit a lone sailing ship approached. It was old as fuck. It appeared deserted. The faded name on the stern was CONCEPCION. They climbed aboard and discovered twelve severely parched and malnourished sailors. At first Les mistook all of them for corpuses. Only they didn't stink like that. Nope they smelled worse. Somebody shit their britches and peed their pants and vomited on their shirts and never cleaned up and never washed their pits for like ever. Les gave them all a salt water rinse.

One of them kept muttering something about that fucking Magellan just had to start a fight with the natives. The bastard. Tara realized she was automatically interpreting Spanish. She rigged up a desalinator out of odds and ends and taped it together with duct tape. Tara is a very resourceful android. She never leaves home without duct tape either. After a bit the de-salinator drooled out enough fresh water to revive the crew. She learned that the ship was one of the five ships Magellan set out from Spain with on the first circumnavigation of the earth. The captain said his name was Gaspar de Quesada. The ship left Spain with 44 crew but lost 4 to scurvy. Three more were beheaded for trying to mutiny. Another was marooned on a deserted island for engaging in homosexual acts with the cabin boy. The cabin boy later jumped overboard in the middle of the ocean. Six were transferred to another ship when they reached the Philippines. One was murdered by the cook for stealing rotten apples from the galley a week before they found the Phillipines. The cook wasn't disciplined but died when he contracted monkeypox from the natives. Maybe it was lumpas lumpess. Anyway he got big welts all over his head and suffocated. How exactly lumps on your head can suffocate someone wasn't completely understood.

Anyway captain Quesada, (don't confuse him with quesa dia, which is something with cheese I think.). Cap. Quesada sent six men ashore to help Magellan quell a native uprising and they were shiskabobbed and roasted on a spit over a bonfire.

Quesada had enough of following that idiot Magellan around the world and shot the bastard in the head when he tried to climb aboard the Concepcion to

escape the natives. Then when the other captains on the other ships said they were going to hang around a bit and rob Chinese junks, Quesada told them to get fucked. He set sail for South America and eventually home to Spain. Unfortunately he sailed against the trade winds that were heading west so he made little headway. Some more crewmen succumbed to the elements and dehydration and starvation and chickenpox they picked up from infected chickens they had brought aboard for provisions. I suspect something was kinky with those chickens. They probably ate seagull shit off the poop deck.

Tara and Les digested this story while they fed the surviving crew a gruel made out of leather belts soaked a day in seawater and fish head and guts from some foolish flying fish that had plopped onto the deck. Three more men croaked during the night from food poisoning. Those old leather belts must have been rotten.

Gaspar de Quesada slipped into a deep state of delusion which was just as well because a couple of the crew said the man was a fucking liar and a fornicator and had been held prisoner in the brig ever since the ship had left the port of St. Julian way back in Argentina. Other crew members claimed that some of their mates were seen nibbling on finger bones of the deceased. Discontent ran rampart. Everyone blamed everyone else for everything that had gone wrong during the voyage. Les had a notion to throw the whole ungrateful bunch overboard. Noe of then expressed thanks for him and Tara saving their lives. They even grumbled when Les insisted they wash their hands after wiping their butts with their hands (No toilet paper was aboard) after doing number two from the poop deck. Tara ignored them. She figured they all

were brain damaged from too much time in the hot sun. This was definitely not a pleasure cruise.

One thing was for certain. Les and Tara were back on Earth in the middle of the Pacific aboard an old Spanish ship and the year was 1520 probably, or close enough for government work.
Les figured this beat the hell out of where they had just been. He spirits picked up more when a rain squal dumped bucket loads of drinking water on them along with some more stupid flying fish. What's with these fish anyway? They have a built in death wish? Anyway he treated the crew to a Friday night fish fry. Who cares if it really wasn't Friday.

The days sailed by. Tara set a course north westward that eventually intercepted winds headed toward the Hawaiian Islands. Les kept them fed by diving for fish that were traveling along with the ship using it as a floating reef. The crew grew stronger and then they began wondering about Les and Tara. How in the world could two people be out swimming in the middle of the ocean with no boat around. They concluded Tara must be a water nymph sent to lure them to Captain Nemo's water world of horrors. Well maybe not exactly but they were mightily suspicious of her. Superstitious fools also believed having a woman aboard was bad luck. Les, they just figured him for a dumbass along for the ride.

Meanwhile Tara confided to Les that the whole setup was suspicious. She consulted her historic archives and found out that the real Captain Gaspar de

Quesada was executed by Magellan for mutiny back in Argentina. She also discovered that the Concepcion was scuttled and burnt up and sunk and abandoned in the Philippines after the Magellan expedition suffered too many casualties and didn't have enough men to man three ships. All of these crewmen were fakes and liars. What the heck was going on here!

Les said somebody must have been here ahead of them and changed history. Another time traveler. Oh wow! Maybe Red is here. Remember Red aka Flaming hair that rides hard from 1876? Also known as Sara.

Whatever the real story was, it all came to a head one night. Tara had shut down for some internal maintenance. Thusly, she appeared to be in a deep sleep to anyone observing her. Les was manning the helm. He was also thinking about Flaming Hair that Rides Hard and how it would be kinda nice to run into her again. The rotten crew crept up on him while he was daydreaming and beat him about the head and shoulders with billy clubs. They would have preferred sticking him in the gizzard with dirks but Tara had thrown all the sharp and pointy things overboard the night before. Things looked dim for Les after he got knocked in the noggin at least sixteen times. Then he got socked in the gut a few dozen times. Then they kicked him in the butt some more times and pulled his hair and poked fingers in his eyes and beat his head against the deck. Then they all took turns jumping on his chest. After about fifteen minutes of beating the crap out of him they were all tuckered out. Les was pretty much dazed but then one of them said, "Lets throw the dumbass overboard."

Nothing revives Les faster than getting called a dumbass. He jumped up. He slugged one in the face, he kicked another in the nuts, he punched one in the gut, he knocked two of their heads together. Les knocked every last one of them senseless. Then he threw the whole lot overboard.

Tara woke up a couple hours later. "Hey Les, anything happening?"
"Nope. Everyone went swimming. "
"Really? I thought none of them could swim."
"Guess somebody shoulda reminded them. Sharks probably ate them all by now."
"Gee what a shame. We are only a few hours from sighting Hawaii. I was planning to throw all of them into a volcano as an offering to the time warp goddess."
"That was a good plan."
"Instead I think we should scuttle this ship in deep water so it's never found again. No sense in screwing up the history books."

Much later.

Tara and Les were resting on the beach. The Concepcion was in a thousand feet of water miles offshore. Suddenly a giant lightning filled waterspout erupted out of the surf and headed toward them.
"Hey Les Look, It's our ride outta here."
"I hope we end up somewhere familiar. And has toilet paper."

They were engulfed by the swirling storm and sucked upward right into the mouth of an erupting volcano.

This could be the end. Or it could be the beginning of a barbecue. Stay tuned.

WHOPPERS AND MORE

LES appeared out of a cloud of smoke. The first thing he noticed was a big Double Whopper with a large order of Fries in front of him. The next thing he noticed was an old man patting him on the shoulder and saying excuse me son but you're sitting in my seat and that's my burger. I just went to get some napkins and poof, here you is.

"Sorry man. Guess I forgot what seat was mine."

Les got the hell outa there before he got tempted to take a bite and run.

Tara was outside waiting for him.

"You just get here?" He asked.

"Nope. I dropped in a few minutes ago right in that same spot, only I had the good sense to get up and leave before that old man left for napkins."

"Where the heck are we now?"

"I'm working on it. Tell me something. What was the last thing you thought about before we got sucked into the waterspout and dumped into a volcano?"

"That really happened huh."

“Yep. Good thing we were traveling at the speed of light or we mighta got scorched.”
“Oh wow! I was thinking about eating a double whopper with fries. Gee, I wonder if that old guy told them to hold the mayo.”
“Uh huh. I thought so. And what were you thinking just before we got sucked out of creepland just before the planets collided.”
“I was thinking about having a big drink of water.”
“Yeah, and we landed in the ocean. Do you see a pattern emerging here?”

Les thought back. Okay in the beginning just before Tara dumped him into the vat full of turnip juice back on the spaceship he remembered thinking it would be nice to see green grass and blue skies and feel real dirt under his feet. Then he woke up in Montana during the Indian Wars. Hold on, what the heck was he thinking about just before that lightning storm whisked them away from 1876 Montana. Oh yeah, just before the lightning vortex thing got them, static electricity made his skin tingle and his hair stand on end and some dust blew into his eyes and he thought— ***Man, what could suck worse than this.*** **And sure enough they landed in dust choked Creepland with killer roaches and shit eaters.**
Les figured next time he would think about———.
“HOLD IT RIGHT THERE BUSTER! THAT’S NOT HAPPENING.
Opps. Apparently Tara could once again read his thoughts.

That’s when that old man come out of the Burger King and handed Les a sack full of Whoppers, extra pickles and mustard, no mayo.

"Here you go young fella, you look like you could eat something. Bet you haven't had a Whopper in a long time. Then the old guy slapped a twenty dollar bill in his hand and told him he might want to buy a new pair of jeans. The ones he had on looked like they came through an Indian war or worse. Then he looked at Tara and pulled out a fifty dollar bill and gave it to her. "Here you go pretty lady. You won that bet." He chuckled and strolled away.

"What bet?"

"I bet that old man that some hungry looking tramp wearing a pair of dirty ripped up calvary troopers trousers would appear out of a cloud of smoke and sit in his place and drool over his double whopper before he came back with his napkins. You showed up right on time."

"Was the sack full of burgers and the twenty part of the bet."

"Nope, guess he figured you needed some help."

"Good, cause I'm not sharing."

"Good cause I don't like whoppers."

"That's cause you don't have to eat."

"Yeah, lucky me."

"Any idea where and when we are?"

"Yep."

"Well?"

"I'm not telling."

"Aww come on."

"Nope. It's my secret."

"Where we going anyway?"

"To find Elon Musk."

"Why?"

"Because he just sold PayPal for millions of dollars and I need to convince him to start Space X and invest in Tesla."

"So you don't exist yet."

"Nope but you do Les and you're going to help me."

"How?"

"It's a secret. Right now we need new clothes. Especially you. Your butt is hanging out of those Calvary britches."

They found the nearest goodwill store and in the used but not abused clothing section found matching jeans and t-shits. The shirts had *I'M NOT LOST, I'M JUST WANDERING* stenciled on the front. Les figured that was better than Tara's first choice of I'M WITH DUMMY for her and DAZED AND CONFUSED for him. That took care of his $20. There was some change left over but Tara bought Les an all day sucker with it.

After that she made him wait outside while she picked up a few things in a few other second hand stores. She also made him promise to not talk to anyone. While he waited, strangers kept stopping and patting him on the back and handing him dollar bills. *What the hell is this?* Finally he noticed a note stuck on his back. It read, "Please help, I'm deaf and dumb and homeless and desperately need a beer." *Now why did I never think of this.* In no time he had collected enough for a tall frosty one.

Tara finished shopping. She emerged from the final store with a backpack full of some things. She wasn't telling what things. She took Les to the nearest

bar and ordered a Bud for him. A tall frosty one. While he sipped his drink she handed him a few essentials which included sunglasses, a straw cowboy hat, a big red bandana, a baseball, a sling shot with a sack of half inch diameter steel ball bearings, a penlight, a multitool , a roll of duct-tape and a lighter.

He looked confused. She told him that all would be revealed in due time. Meanwhile Les consulted what remained of his stellar memory. The Bud helped. Lets see, Elon Musk sold PayPal in 2002 and pocketed about 180 million bucks.

"It's 2002 isn't it!"

"Very good. You aren't always a dumb ass Les."

Was that a compliment.

"Now where are we?"

Les looked around. He ventured a guess. California?

"What tipped you off?"

"All the cars have California plates."

"Wow, keep this up and I'll buy you another beer."

"I bought this one."

"I put the sign on your back so you could afford it."

As Les sipped his second Bud, Tara outlined her plan.

Step 1. Find Elon. This was going to be easy. Tara had a *find Elon* app. In her files. He was currently 11 miles away. Then she used the CIA's presently secret program named EARTH VIEWER to zoom in on his exact location.

Earth viewer was the precurser to Google Earth which hadn't been invented yet.
Step 2. Kidnap Elon. She told Les the plan. He wasn't thrilled. She told him tough shit.
Step 3. convince Elon to start his own space exploration company and he should call it Space X.
Step 4. Get outta dodge before the cops arrived.

Les donned his disguise. That consisted of wearing the straw cowboy hat and the dark sunglasses and pulling the bandana up over his mouth like an old time stagecoach robber. (If you recall back in 2002 Les was an unknown dumb ass from Montana. He was known to try to beat up bullies that picked on people, mostly unsuccessfully. Hence the dumb ass moniker.). What that has to do with this story , I have no idea.

Tara stationed them along a seldom used back road she knew Elon would be driving on shortly. How did she know she wouldn't say except Elon was being lured there for a meeting/ rendezvous/ game of marbles or whatever.
"Okay Les you do step 2, the kidnapping. I do step 3."
"Why me?"
"Because I can't be seen because Elon hasn't built me yet."
Elon's car appeared. Les stepped out in front of it. Elon Stepped on the gas. He had just completed a defensive driving course on how to thwart highwaymen. Don't stop for masked men was lesson number one. Run the bastard over was lesson number two.

Les was prepared. He threw the baseball through Elons windshield. Elon skidded to a stop. Les pulled out his slingshot and shot holes in the car's radiator. Elon locked the doors. Les used his multitool lock pick to open the drivers door. Then he put Elon into a headlock until Elon cried uncle. Then he duct taped Elons arms and legs and mouth and eyes. Then he threw Elon over his shoulder and carried him to the waiting van that Tara had borrowed from a used car lot. She drove them to a deserted cabin in the woods. She found it through Zillow and reconnoitered it with Earth Viewer. All of which was on Google. Funny name, great idea. No wonder it would eventually catch on until everyone googled.

Now Tara began step 3. She used her telepathic comms to enlighten him of a few things. Elon was receptive to telepathic communication as a result of mind enhancing exercises he indulged in while growing up.
First off Tara tried to convince him to stop thinking about creating a social media internet company because some dink named Zuckerberg was all over that idea. Same with another thing where idiot politicians could vent one sentence nonsense in tweets. No, no Elon, go with your childhood dreams of building rocket ships and space exploration. Then she told him how he could do space rockets on the cheap. *Make them reusable.*

Fantastic idea. Elon figured he had thought of it himself.
Next agenda. Make electric cars. Tara fed him all the positive facts about EV's. Another fantastic idea he figured was originally his. Then she convinced him to invest in a fledging company called TESLA which was

trying to do that. She also convinced him to buy as many shares as he could and corner as many options as possible. When she showed him how that would make him a billionaire he was sold.

Finally she fed him ideas on artificial intelligence and robotics. He was skeptical. She ripped off his blindfold.

"Look at me asshole. I'm a robot chuck full of artificial intelligence. She then demonstrated a few of her talents. He realized there was something to the idea. But she scared the crap out of him because she could do anything a human could do only better. Visions of the Terminator movies sprang to mind. This is when he got an idea of his own—any robot he built would have to have a built in mandate to harm no human.

Tara was finished. Les took over. He shined his penlight into Elons eyes until he was dazed and bewildered. Then he smacked him in the head and knocked him cold. While he was out, Les returned him to his car and removed all the duct tape. Then he and Tara got the hell outta dodge.

Elon came to just as a highway cop pulled up.

"What happened here buddy."

"Some asshole threw a baseball through my windshield. Guess it hit me in the head and I blacked out."

The cop put out an APB on a baseball throwing asshole. Elon went about his business with a couple great ideas. Reusable rockets made of stainless steel, automatic robotic manned assembly lines, gigi-factories, starlight

communication satellite network, etc, etc. Then he went looking for a start up something called Tesla.
Eventually He looked at the baseball. It was autographed by some dumb ass named Les Didlin. Man what a dumb name. Bet that bozo never gets laid much.

A few hours later and a few more miles away. Tara and Les began a long distance thru hike on the Pacific Crest trail. Tara figured that was as good a place as any to run into another time warp portal. She might be right because the trail crosses some high ridges where intense lightning storms occasionally occur.

They traveled the trail clear to Washington state. Plenty of lightning storms crossed their path. None of them contained a time warp portal. Tara concluded they might be stuck in 2002 for a while. Which might be interesting. She convinced Les to go to Redmond and check out the job situation there. First they had to walk through Seattle. They were down near the waterfront, broke and Les was hungry. Then he noticed something going on at a street corner. Cars were pulling up and stopping next to a suspicious looking guy. He handed them a little package, the occupants handed him cash. Hmm, thought Les.
"Tara, wait for me at the Fish Market. I got an errand to run."
She went on ahead. Les approached the street corner guy.
"Hey buddy, can you spare a buck. I really need a beer."
"Get the fuck outta here bozo."

“Come on, your pocket is full of cash. A couple bucks won’t hurt you.”

The guy pulled a switchblade. “Beat it asshole.”

Les swatted the knife away. Then he punched the guy in the stomach.

The guy staggered back. Then he pulled out a little 25 cal. Automatic.

“You asked for it Dumb Ass.” He pulled the trigger just as Les pushed the barrel down. The bullet hit the guy in the foot. Then Les socked him in the mouth. “That’s for pulling a gun on me.” Then he kneed the guy in the balls. “That’s for calling me a dumb ass.”

Then he pulled the guy into an ally and stripped him naked and threw him in a dumpster.

A bit later Les met Tara at the fish market. “Where have you been Les?”

“Just cleaning up the streets a bit. Look here, some guy loaned me a wad of money.”

“Do we need to get outta town real quick?”

“Wouldn’t hurt.”

A few hours later. And a change of clothes from Goodwill. And a beer and a bean and cheese burrito for Les. They were in Redmond. At a Starbucks.

“Ok Les, we need to find jobs. You can’t be rolling drug dealers here.”

“How did you know?”

“I can read your mind, remember. And let me tell you bud. It aint happening.”

“What?”

“What you think about 99 percent of the time.”

Oh that thing.”

"Now think about getting a job. Meet me here at midnight."

Les searched here and there. He searched high and low. He searched uptown and downtown and all around the town. Then he searched outside of town. Eventually he found a job shoveling shit at a chicken farm. Seemed like dejavue was happening all over again. *If you dedicated Les Didlin fans remember, his first job was shoveling shit at a diary farm.* He was just happy he didn't get the chicken plucking job. There were a couple chickenshit assholes working there.

***T*ara did better. Much better. She landed a job with Microsoft and joined the team working to upgrade Windows. Boy did she have some ideas that were 20 years ahead of everyone else. Some other less talented employees started to resent her. After all they were merely human.**

A few weeks passed. Les was promoted to the head shit shoveler position. That meant they gave him a bigger shit shovel in a bigger chicken barn. He was less than ecstatic. It seems he got promoted ahead of the lead chicken plucker who was in line for the job. Chicken shit shovelers pay scale started a cent and a half above chicken pluckers. Not much but the head shit shoveler position came with an added perk. You got to take home all the chicken shit you wanted. That chicken plucker vowed revenge. Tensions at the job increased.

At Microsoft the managers figured Tara would be more suited to the space cadet team since her ideas were so far out there for normal nearsighted people. She was put in charge of creating the next generation of X-BOX realistic action games. She developed 'Mars Explorer'. It didn't catch on

because the main character was a know it all android. But the 'Legend of Zelda' did. Too bad that was an Nintendo game. Next she worked on 'Dumb, Armed and Dangerous' which was inspired by her adventures with Les.

Everything appeared to be hunky dory which was less than ideal but mostly tolerable with our two time travelers. But danger lurked in the cosmos. It all started when Tara was required to take a surprise physical for medical coverage at work. She said she didn't want or need medical coverage. They said tough shit, it's required. That's when it was discovered she had no pulse. Then they found out she wasn't breathing either. Concerned medical staff subjected her to a whole battery of other tests. Then they tried to get a blood sample. Androids don't have blood. They don't have a pulse much less a beating hearth and they sure as hell don't breathe. She was whisked off to the medical research center by the security team. She was put in a room filled with stuff used for autopsies. Medical experts were concerned. They consulted scientists working on artificial insemination. No that's not right. These experts were studying artificial intelligence.

Tara was more concerned they were going to open her up to see what made her tick. Tara slipped out a back door and ran. Just in time to evade some government officials tasked with investigating weird shit and or aliens. These guys were from secret department call The X-Files. Then somebody realized she was probably a robot. An all points bulletin was sent out. She was wanted for impersonating a human and suspected of spying for a foreign entity or an alien race.

Tara collected Les who was knee deep in chicken shit.

"Hey amigo, it's time to get outa Dodge. These people don't respect the rights of humanoid androids. There are some morons after me who intend to do an autopsy on me."

They took off for the woods. Just in time because somebody, most likely a disgruntled chicken plucker, had recognized Les as a fugitive wanted for kidnapping Elon Musk. Apparently Elon had hired a sketch artist from Disneyland to illustrate his kidnapper. In all honesty the sketch looked more like Goofy Dog with a straw hat and sunglasses. The one million dollar reward offered for information leading to his arrest sparked a couple thousand tips but the most plausible led to a chicken shit shoveler in Redmond Washington. The sheriff dispatched his squat team to check it out. (Note this was a squat team, not to be confused with a swat team.) Swat teams kick down doors and shoot people. Squat teams drive around with sirens blazing and sit in their cruisers eating jelly doughnuts after turning a pack of dogs loose to run down the suspect.

Les and Tara went running through the woods. A pack of vicious killer beagles were hot on their heels. Fortunately The sheriff's pack of pitbulls was currently chasing down a jaywalker on the other side of the county. So he called in the second team. Luckily they were available because the third team was made up of man eating chihuahuas. Les hated the little barking bastards.

Les led Tara into an underbrush choked canyon. They ran through the bushes and they ran through the brambles , they ran so fast that the beagles couldn't catch them.

Just then a swirling hot pink cloud moved in and coated everything in the canyon in cotton candy. This was vertically unpresendent . Correction: it was un-presendented, oh fuck; it never happened before okay. About that time a truck loaded with powdered sugar was struck by lightning just as it collided with a truck carrying pink food coloring and a extremely rare giant whirlwind sucked everything into the stratosphere. Okay that's one plausible explanation for the cotton candy storm. Then a conflagration disguised as a purple people eater gobbled up Les and Tara. Sorry, I have no explanation for this. They were whisked through time and space to who knows where. On the way Tara told Les to think of something familiar. She didn't want to end up in a deserted wasteland again.

Desert wasteland

Some time passed. Tara and Les were tumbled around in a swirling vortex of gaseous vapors. Les said, "Opps that one slipped out."

Eventually the sky opened and they hit the ground in a torrential downpour, also know as a monsoon in Arizona.

The rain quit. Tara looked around. They were in a deserted wasteland! She socked Les in the shoulder. "What the hell were you thinking?"

"You wanted someplace familiar, this is it."

Tara consulted her geolocation time distillery. "Holy crap, we're in the middle of the U.S. Army's Desert Training Center in 1942. This is where General

Patton trained troops for combat in North Africa. She checked their exact coordinates. "

"Okay Les, you ever been on Cunningham Mountain just southwest of Quartzite Arizona."

"Hmm, oh yeah. That's when I was practicing to be a hermit."

"How'd that work out?"

"It didn't. The damn snowbirds kept bothering me."

Les looked around. They were up near the summit at over 3000 feet. He spotted a big dust cloud to the northwest. Tara zoomed in with her telescopic vision.

"That's a tank column from the 3rd armor division out practicing maneuvers. Opps, hold on they stopped. Oh for crying out loud. The bastards are shooting this way."

Soon tank rounds starting exploding on the slopes below them. The rounds crept up the mountainside.

"I think we better move Les."

"I know where to go, follow me."

Les ran off around a rock formation that looked suspiciously like a big target. One with a big bullseye painted on it. They climbed higher, right past other things that could have been mockups of German tanks. They didn't notice, somehow???

"Where we going?"

"The old Yum Yum gold mine is around here. We can hide in the main tunnel."

A few minutes later they reached the mine entrance and dashed inside. Almost immediately several tank rounds scored direct hits on the mine entrance. When the dust cleared they found the mine entrance blocked by tons of rock.

“Son of a gun. Who knew this was their target.”

“Way to go dumb ass. There another way out?”

“Maybe, I think, I hope.”

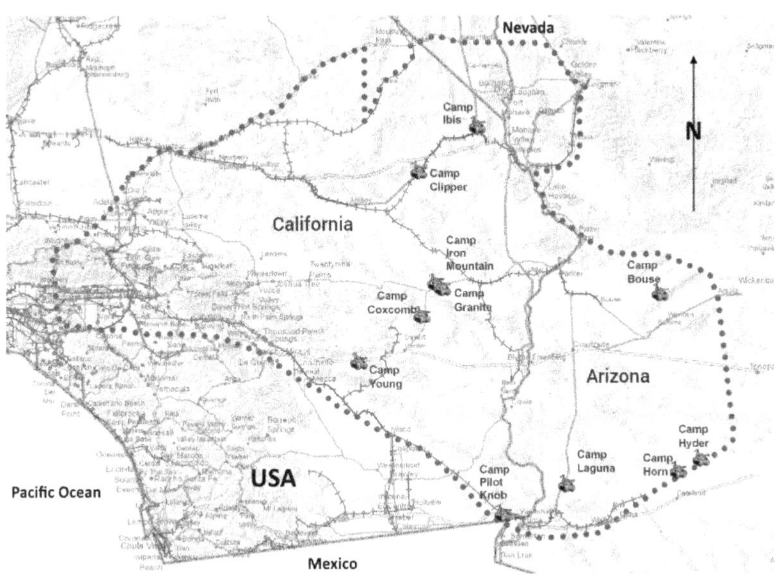

The Desert Training Area covered a big area including parts of California, Arizona and Nevada.

Les led the way through a maze of shafts and tunnels. He still had his penlight to show the way. Tara suddenly stopped him.
"When did this mine close Les?"
"I think at the start of WWII. The government closed all non-strategic mining operations. Especially low producing gold mines like this."
" So around 1941-1942. I guess they just up and left everything behind."
"Probably."
"Including these cases of refried beans and cheese and tortillas? "
"Wow. We can make bean and cheese burritos. I won't starve while you find a way out of here."
"That is your job, remember."

Suddenly they were both blinded by a powerful strobe light. Then hundreds of little yellow pudgy things wearing bib overalls and goggles surrounded them. There were all armed with picks and shovels and baseball bats and fireplace pokers and axes and knives and pitchforks and meat cleavers and rolling pins and tire wrenches and screwdrivers and cresent wrenches and hammers and pooper scoopers and brooms.
One of them came up to Les and looked him over. Then he turned to his fellows and said, "Relax guys, I know this one. He's harmless."

"Stuart!"

"Yeah, it's me Les, your little yellow pudgy buddy. About time you got here and who is your charming companion?"

Les introduced Tara. She appeared skeptical. Minions? Really! Then she pointed to Stuart.

"Why does he have only one eye?"

"Genetics. Minions that have only one eye have a foot long pecker so it's an even trade off."

"Oh yeah, well tell him to keep that pecker in his pants or I'll poke his other eye out."

Stuart reminded Les that minions also have foot long tongues.

Tara said the little fucker was pushing it. She still had that mandate to harm no human but it didn't apply to puny little yellow bastards.

Les explained the situation to Stuart. "She can read your mind little buddy and she doesn't fool around, even with little one eyed guys with foot long dongs."

"Dang."

Les and Stuart traded stories on how come they had ended up here in this old mine. You already know Les's story, implausible as it is. This is Stuart's. You might remember when Earth and Theia collided. Well the minions lived on Theia. They got sucked up in a giant time warp wormhole thing-a-ma-jig just in time and have been time and space travelers ever since. Also minions live almost forever so Stuart has seen it all and then some. About a year and a half ago Stuart and some of his buddies got sent (teleported) here to the Yum Yum mine. It wasn't always named the Yum Yum. Before they got here it was

called the witches shit hole. Apparently the previous owners were disgruntled after spending all their money operating this mine and only finding enough gold to fill a couple teeth. They were superstitious old coots and thought an old hag that lived in a nearby HoHo Kum pueblo was a witch that had cursed them because they caught her taking a dump in the mine shaft. They abandoned the place soon there-after.

The minions started growing magic mushrooms that were real yummy. Probably fertilized by the witches shit. Then the army moved into the area and General Patton confiscated the mushrooms. He didn't believe in witches shit or curses. In exchange he gave the minions permission to run a food truck throughout the sprawling military base. The only restrictions were no magic mushrooms, buy war bonds with 50 percent of the profits and don't screw the troops. So Stuart started importing beans and cheese and corn tortillas from Sonora and sold bean and cheese burritos and cold beer from the food truck.

He showed Les and Tara the food truck. It was hidden in the mine near the lower exit tunnel during the day. It only came out at night to service off duty personnel. The truck was spectacular. It was a five ton military truck formerly demolished by a tank round. The minions resurrected it from the scrap heap. The truck pulled a trailer and truck and trailer were all painted in glow in the dark red white and blue stripes. The truck sides had signs showing bean and cheese burritos for a nickel and cold Duff Beer for a dime. Down in a corner in small letter was another sigh that read—fluffy ass wipe -a

buck fifty. As you may know, eating bean and cheese burritos necessitates plenty of ass wipe. Fluffy preferred.

The trailer just had a sign on the side with the letters B J -25 cents.

"What the heck does B J stand for."

Stuart giggled. "General Patton thinks it stands for bread and jam but he told us to keep the troops happy and not screw them."

Tara figured it out. Les remained clueless. Even when he saw the back of the trailer depicting a foot long tongue coming out of a happy face with Yum Yum B Js written under it. Okay, according to Bill Clinton, blow jobs don't count as screwing so the minions weren't breaking Pattons orders. And they were definitely keeping the troops happy.

Then Stuart dropped the bombshell. He explained that the minions had figured out how time travel worked. They had been working on it for over four billion years so it was about time. Then he explained that he had been tracking Les ever since they had split up. Why? Apparently Stuart had been appointed as Les Didlin's personal minion. Which meant Les was his responsibility. Now due to her relationship with Les, Tara also became Stuarts responsibility. When he discovered Les and Tara were *lost in space* he tried to bring them back to earth. Seems that all the kinks hadn't been ironed out so there were a few misfires but now they were here. Tara pointed out that 1942 wasn't exactly *here,* since she and Les left Earth in 2020. Stuart said it was close enough. Besides that he was here and he wanted to do some upgrades on them.

He took Les and Tara to another deep chamber in the mine. All manner of advanced electronic and medical equipment was set up there. It was a unbelievable space age lab. Even Tara couldn't comprehend all the things she saw. Stuart explained. Minions, including Stuart had progressed through time to the year 3000. That meant that for now they couldn't go any further into the future but they could go back anywhere in time older than the year 3000. The minions were privy to all the advances in everything up to 3000 so of course Tara wouldn't know about that stuff. Mind blowing isn't it?

Then Stuart pulled out a mind dazzler fog pistol and shot them both in the butt. Whatever was in the fog pistol affects both humans and androids which meant they were incapacited. With one minor exception. Les also crapped his pants because his asshole wasn't incapacitated. Tara didn't- probably because androids don't eat therefore don't crap. Sure saves them from buying toilet paper.

Apparently the upgrades Stuart had in mind didn't require willing participants. Then while they were dazed and confused and mostly immobilized he turned them over to the minion lab techs. Who wish to remain annynonomouos at least until the statute of limitations runs out. Some time passed. Who knows how much time since minions don't wear watches or look at calenders because they never run out of time, or take time off.

Repairs and upgrades were eventually completed. Stuart slapped a final inspection tag on their foreheads. Then he ran them both through the power wash and wax machine and they came out all shiny and squeaky clean.

A couple hours later Les and Tara awoke. Stuart told them it was time. He put them in a glass chamber and asked them what, where and when they wanted to be.

"This is most likely irreversible and probably the very last time you guys will ever be transported anywhere else so make it good."

Les didn't have a clue. So many choices. The very thought of it made him dizzy dazed and confused. Hmm, no apparent upgrade in that department.

Tara consulted the technicians. She questioned Stuart. He agreed with some suggestions she made. Finally when she was completely satisfied she said they were ready. Stuart pulled a switch. Tara and Les vanished. No smoke, no lightning, no sonic booms or hurricane force winds or swirling gas clouds. Just POOF!

SOMEWHERE, SOMEPLACE, SOMETIME

Les was in a deep coma induced brain fog. Then the fog lifted.

They re-materialized. Les looked at Tara. Then he looked at himself.

Holy crap! Tara, You got us turned into ***PREDATORS.***

RELAX LES. These are just time traveler space suits. Nothing can harm us when we wear them. Except maybe real Predators but those guys mostly hang out on the other side of the galaxy.

WHERE are we going?

It's a surprise. So hold on, things might get bumpy.

Things proceeded to get bumpy. Especially inside the predator suits. Apparently the minions installed some alliterating gizmos inside those suits. Whoever put them on wouldn't come out exactly the same as before donning the suits. Boy were they gonna be surprised. Les was for sure. Maybe even mystified.

THE END

STAY TUNED FOR FUTURE EPISODES OF LES AND TARA TIME TRAVELER ADVENTURES WHICH MAY BE FORTHCOMING IN THE NEAR FUTURE. Or the past if you are another time traveler because you can't go to your future until time has past.

Whew, now I'm mystified.

PS: don't hold your breath, this might take awhile. De-mystification might take time.

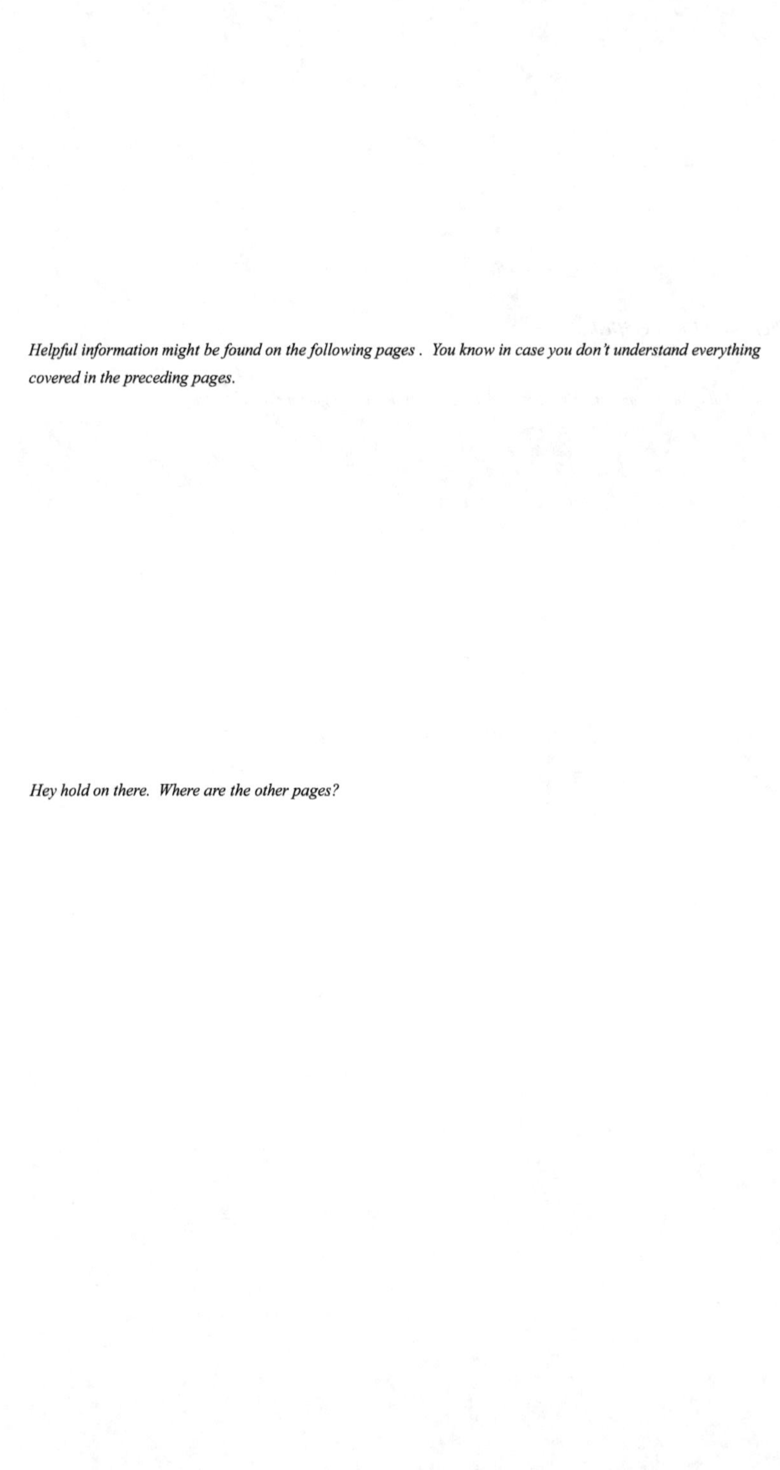

Helpful information might be found on the following pages . You know in case you don't understand everything covered in the preceding pages.

Hey hold on there. Where are the other pages?

Excerpt from.

THE SCALAWAG SHENANIGINS

Les surfaced. He was in a lagoon, about thirty feet from shore. Light from a large hotel/resort reflected off the water surface. Everything was quiet. Tara had gone on ahead to make sure. He slowly dog paddled to the sandy beach. There he stripped off his predator suit down to shorts and t-shirt. Quickly he scurried under the shadows of nearby towering palm trees. So far so good. He made his way to the side entrance and waited. Finally the delivery driver pulled into the driveway. Les hurried over.

“You the Uber Treats guy?”

“Yea mon, got an order of one dozen happy meals, a quarter pounder with cheese, two big macs, two large orders of fries, and two large sprites. That will be $37.89.”

“Put it on the Mar Largo tab.”

“Nu un, cash only, the bozo that lives here done stiffed me before. Aint no Mar Largo account no mo.”

Les dug into his wallet. All he had was two tens and a fifty. He handed the fifty dollar bill over.

“Thanks mon.”

“I need some change.”

"Sorry mon, don't carry no change." The driver sped off.

Les entered the delivery entrance. A hand reached out of the shadows and grabbed him.

"Damn it Tara! You almost made me crap my pants."

"Relax. The coast is clear. Put these clothes on." She haded him a waiters outfit.

Les did as he was told. Better to not know where the clothes came from or who she took them off of or how. (Tara no longer operated under the *harm no human mandate).*

While he dressed, she added a special condiment to the food.

She grinned. "Guess what Les, we lucked out. Ted Cruz is dining with fat ass tonight. He gets the quarter pounder. I gave it an extra dose.

She faded back into the shadows. Not that she needed much fading since she was wearing her nearly invisible predator suit. Les took the food to the dining room. Two assholes sat opposite each other. One resembled an obese hog. The other a slimy rat. One was picking his nose and eating it. The other was scratching his balls with one hand and smoothing down his combover with the other. He switched hands frequently. Les set the food down between them and hurried out the door. "Hey shit for brains, bring some ketchup."

"Oh fuck, where do they keep the ketchup?"

A hand shot out of the shadows and handed him a bottle of ketchup. Tara was always ahead of the game. He delivered the ketchup and practically ran for the door.

Back outside. They waited in the shadows. Three minutes passed. Then five. Then they heard running down the hallway. A door slammed shut. Then pounding on the door. *Let me in. Find another toilet. I gotta go. Tough shit, my house, my John. Go fuck yourself.* Then more running. Then a gosh awful gushing sound, followed by a horrific stench that permeated the whole compound. Just then Ted came bursting out the door. He was holding both hands over his fat ass while he shuffled toward his car. Then he let out a massive groan and shit all over himself. It was like a spouting geyser.

"Time to leave."

"Yep, our job is done."
Back on the beach Les slipped back into his predator suit and instantly became nearly invisible. Les and Tara slipped back into the lagoon. They ducked under and swam away.

Stuart monitored the events from the super secret minion spy satellite high overhead. Cruz left a slimy shit trail all the way to the airport. Then he was forced to get hosed off before the crew let him board his airplane.. They had to jettison forty pounds of shit over Dallas. The crew almost threw Ted out after mistaking him for a giant turd. Ted was confined to the shitter for three weeks once he got home. People still mistook him for a giant turd.

Back at Mar a Largo, fat ass Donald shit himself stupid for three months. All the toilets overflowed. The ballroom floor turned into a shit slide. The shitting was just one inconvenient thing. Tara had switched his Trump brand asshole grease butt cream to a concoction of itching powder and hot pepper sauce. And his toilet paper was replaced by asbestos infused wipe. His asshole got so ripped raw he had to have a pigs butthole transplant.
For the remainder of his pathetic existence he had to wear extra absorbent obese size diapers. Every time he told a lie he experienced a bout of explosive diarrhea. He had to shuffle instead of walk so he could clamp his asshole tight to keep from emitting noxious farts. His circle of friends wafted away.
Stuart consulted his notes. Okay destination number one completed. He flipped the page to destination number two. He laughed. Oh boy. That Tara is a genius. This will be epic.

Tara shook Les awake. "Come on lazybones, we're here. What's with the crazy grin. You been having another wet dream or something."
Les pried his eyes open. He looked at Tara. What the hell? He looked at himself. Something was really screwy.
"Did we just leave Stuart back in 1942 at the Yum Yum mine?"

“Yep.”

“This is our first stop.”

“Yep.”

“Man did I just have a crazy dream. You sure we didn’t make a stop at Mar a Largo and pull some shenanigans on Donald Trump.”

“No other stops Les. This is it, our destination.”

Les just realized something. He looked again to double check.

“YOU GOT US TURNED INTO MINIONS!!!

“Yep. You notice anything else?” She held up a mirror.

“Yeah, I only got one eye.”

“Yep. Anything special about minions with one eye?’

“You’re kidding me.”

“Nope, check it out.” Les checked it out.

HOLY SHIT.

“HEY get your hand outa my pants.”

“Oh my gosh!”

The end

Finally!   Thank gosh

Other Les Didlin adventures you may not enjoy:

THE NOOKIE FILE

THE SUPERSTITION FILE

THE SCREWY LOUIE FILR

THE ZOMBIE FILE

THE EASTWOOD FILE

LES DIDLIN VERSES THE IRS

THE PREDATOR FILE

MORE DIDLIN

THE ASININE FILE

THE PHOENIX

WOLF WOMAN

DICKS DICKS

LES DIDLIN RETURNS

LES DIDLIN DESPERADO

About the author:

Will might have come from Montana and then when he was old enough to know better he immigrated to Arizona where several decades of hot dry sunny days raisenifided his mind. Then he started writing Les Didlin books based loosely on past experiences coupled with a fertilized mind.

Les Didlin fans might reach him at lesdidlin@yahoo.com
Then again they might not since that might be a phony address and will sanders might be a phony name. However to make sure another dumbass Les Didlin novel never gets born, concerned citizens might send generous donations to that phony address with pleas to STOP.

ADIOS

www.ingramcontent.com/pod-product-compliance
Lightning Source LLC
LaVergne TN
LVHW050323160826
845677LV00014B/3519

* 9 7 9 8 3 6 1 2 0 1 3 9 6 *